The high VOYAGE

Olga Litowinsky

The hIGh VOYAGE

The Final Crossing of Christopher Columbus

Delacorte Press

Published by
Delacorte Press
Bantam Doubleday Dell Publishing Group, Inc.
666 Fifth Avenue
New York, New York 10103

This edition was first published in 1977 by The Viking Press.

Library of Congress Cataloging in Publication Data

Litowinsky, Olga.
    The high voyage / Olga Litowinsky.
      p. cm.
    Summary: Fernando Columbus recounts his eventful voyage with
his father in search of a passage to India.
    ISBN 0-385-30304-1
    1. Columbus, Christopher—Juvenile fiction. 2. Colón,
Fernando, 1488–1539—Juvenile fiction. 3. America—Discovery
and exploration—Fiction. [1. Columbus, Christopher—Fiction.
2. Columbus, Ferdinand, 1488–1539—Fiction. 3. Adventure and
adventurers—Fiction.] I. Title.
PZ7.L698Hi 1991
[Fic]—dc20   90-37722
                                       CIP
                                       AC

Manufactured in the United States of America

April 1991

10 9 8 7 6 5 4 3 2 1

BVG

In memory of my mother & father,
who also crossed the Ocean Sea

Contents

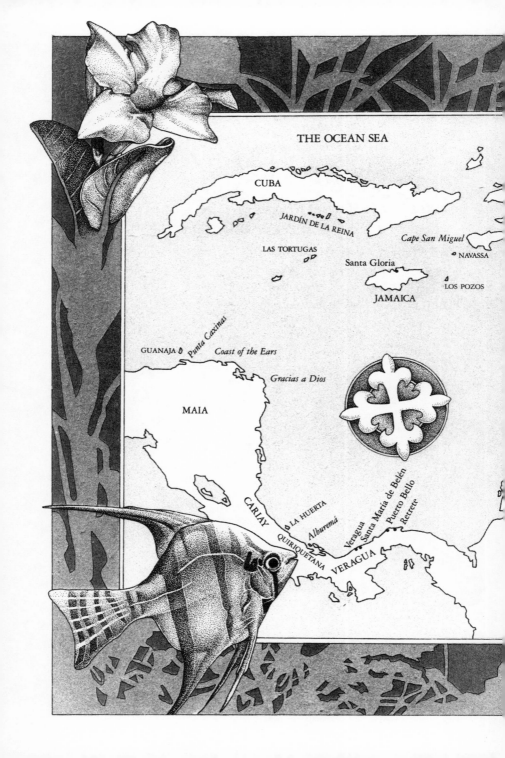

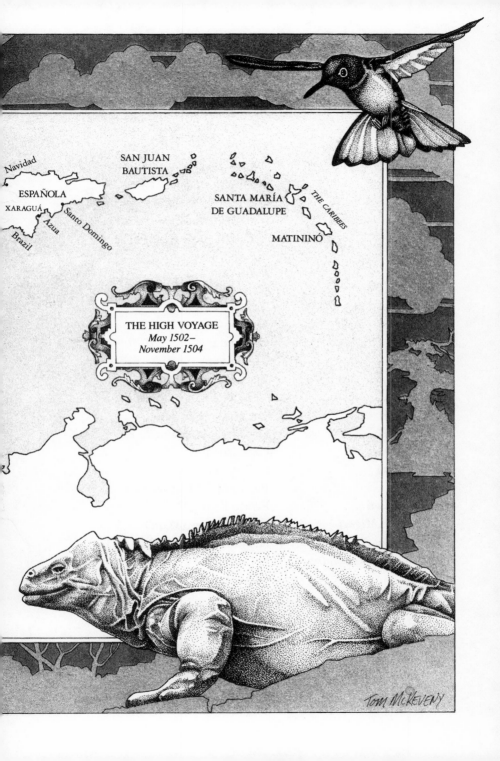

Navidad

SAN JUAN
BAUTISTA

ESPAÑOLA

XARAGUÁ

Azua   Santo Domingo

Brazil

SANTA MARÍA
DE GUADALUPE

THE CARIBBEES

MATININÓ

THE HIGH VOYAGE
*May 1502–
November 1504*

Tom McKeveny

AS USED BY FERNANDO	MODERN EQUIVALENTS
Alburemá	Chiriquí Lagoon (Panama)
Brazil (Puerto)	Jacmel (Haiti)
Cariay	Puerto Limón (Costa Rica)
Cathay	China
Ciamba	Indochina
Cipangu	Japan
Española	Hispaniola (Haiti and the Dominican Republic)
Guanahani	Watlings Island or San Salvador (Bahamas)
Guanaja	Bonacca
La Huerta (Quiribiri)	Uva Island (Costa Rica)
Las Tortugas	Cayman Islands
Los Pozos	Morant Cays
Maia	In Honduras
Matininó	Martinique
The Ocean Sea	The Atlantic Ocean
Puerto de Bastimentos	Nombre de Dios (Panama)
Puerto Bello	Portobelo (Panama)
Puerto Bueno	Dry Harbour (Jamaica)
Punta Caxinas	Cape Honduras
Quiriquetana	In Panama
Retrete	Puerto de los Escribanos (Panama)
San Juan Bautista	Puerto Rico
(Cabo) San Miguel	Cape Tiburon (Haiti)
Santa Gloria	St. Ann's Bay (Jamaica)
Santa María de Guadalupe	Guadeloupe
Veragua	In Panama
Xaraguá	In Haiti

Prologue / *Seville, November 2, 1507*

SO THAT THE BEST PART of the world may know of the events that befell us and of the marvels we saw in the Indies, I herein relate the history of the High Voyage, for so my father, the Admiral Christopher Columbus, called his fourth voyage (and my first) to the Indies, which began in the Year of Our Lord 1502 when I was thirteen.

Part I

I / *Clouds in My Head*

I STOOD IN THE center of the Patio of the Lions, watching the water fall from their carved mouths and listening to the music flow from the fingers of the lutist who had come outside to practice in the early spring sunshine. The melody was sure and pretty, and the lutist began to sing: "How sadly I wander, conquered by love." I knew Her Highness, Queen Isabella, would like this new song. She had been melancholy the past winter in Granada, and the song would fit her mood as it did mine.

As I stared at the lions, not really seeing them, thoughts began to heap in my mind like clouds before a storm. I still had not recovered from being told by my father, only moments before, that I was to go with him to the Indies. Of course I had eagerly agreed: it was only meet that I do so. I am his second son, and someday I shall share in the revenues from all the lands the Admiral Christopher Columbus has taken possession of for their Highnesses, the Catholic Sovereigns of Spain, Ferdinand and Isabella. The voyage was not to be missed: I would see mermaids and cannibals and marvels beyond measure with my own eyes.

Yet his news, like the music, made me feel both happy and sad. I was sorrowful at the thought of leaving the Queen, for she had been as good and kind to me as my own mother. I wondered, was I ready to leave my comfortable life at court to take part in such a long and hazardous venture? My father's wanting me along meant that he believed I was no longer a child. This pleased me, as did the thought that I would come to know him better. I was only four when he returned from his first voyage to the Indies, and he had made two other crossings of the Ocean Sea since then, which meant he had been away for most of my thirteen years.

And what about the gossip I had overheard a few days ago, shortly before my father arrived in Granada? No one at the court thought the Admiral would find the passage to India on his next voyage. Some even said that the Queen had given in to my father's demands only to be rid of a nuisance, whom she secretly wished would never return.

When I had repeated the gossip to my father this morning, he raised his head and clicked his tongue, and began to pace back and forth across the patio impatiently. At last he spoke. "Those envious fools who surround the Queen and try to poison her mind against me are afraid to walk as far as the marketplace, lest they trip over a stone in the road. How can you expect them to understand when I speak of India?" He sounded so angry I was sorry I had mentioned the gossip. All at once he stopped pacing and looked into my eyes.

"I know there is a passage, and it must be followed up. It is certain that if not now, then later some new thing of great value will be found."

He reached into his sleeve and pulled out a scroll covered with the royal seals. "Her Highness believes me. She has never lost her faith in me. See this letter: I am to give it to Vasco da Gama. Listen to what Her Highness has written: 'Since by good hap you may meet by sea, we have commanded Admiral Don Christopher Columbus that if you two meet, you should treat each other as friends.'

"Read it for yourself, Fernando," he said.

I took the letter and looked closely at my father. His hair, which had once been as red as mine, was now silver, but his blue eyes were as keen as always. Reassured by the strength in those eyes, I quickly skimmed over the Queen's letter to the great Portuguese navigator. Perhaps I, too, would meet him on those faraway seas.

"I want you to know that I believe you, Father," I said. "What a glorious day it will be when you hand this letter to da Gama as I am handing it to you now."

The Admiral smiled as he replaced the scroll in his sleeve, and I felt a warmth in my heart. His arm around my shoulders, he walked with me away from the fountain and toward the palace.

"You will soon see the truth of your faith, Fernando," he said with affection and pride in his voice. "One day, like my countryman Marco Polo, we shall ride through the Strait of Malacca, with a high wind behind us and the open road to India before."

We stood together for a moment in the shade of the Moorish arches. My father looked around the cobbled patio, at the lions, the orange trees, and the Arabic writing carved into the walls of the palace.

"You were still a baby the year their Highnesses conquered this stronghold, driving the Moors from Spain forever. A few months later Her Highness made it possible for me to sail to the Indies for the first time. Other Spaniards, the Portuguese, the French, the English—none believed that I, the son of a Genoese weaver, could cross the Ocean Sea and return. The Queen's faith in me and my enterprise at that time was a good omen, Fernando. God will continue to smile on my ventures.

"I must go now, for much remains to be done. Your uncle Bartholomew and I expect to have the preparations for the voyage completed in Seville by late April. I shall let you know where and when to join us—probably in May in Cádiz. Until then God keep you."

The Admiral held my face between his hands and kissed me on the cheeks. We embraced, and then he went into the coolness of the Alhambra. "And God keep you, Father," I whispered. Dazed by all I had heard, I returned to the sun and the sounds of the falling water and the lute.

A peacock approached the fountain. It stood before me, proudly facing the Moorish lions, and spread its tail in a shimmering dark rainbow. The lutist's fingers began to search for a new melody. Was my father right? I wondered. Would this be the High Voyage to India the Admiral dreamed of? I could not bear to doubt any longer.

The clouds in my head began to drift away as I recalled my father's deeds. Had he not already discovered hundreds of islands —Española, Cuba, Jamaica? Had he not already repaid the Queen's faith with gold and pearls and spices? Why shouldn't he reach India this time?

Suddenly it struck me: when he did, I would be at his side.

I ran into the palace to look for my older brother. Would Diego regret that he was not going on the High Voyage to India? Probably not. I slowed down. He was growing stuffier with each year he spent at court, learning its ways so that someday he could protect his—and the family's—interests. It was where he belonged until he stepped into my father's shoes.

I could not hold down my excitement any longer. I jumped into the air, wanting to shout so all should hear: I, Fernando Columbus, am going to cross the Ocean Sea! But since I was still the Queen's page, I walked sedately back to find Diego.

II / *Santa Catalina*

TRUE TO MY father's words, we came aboard the *Capitana*, the flagship of our fleet, at Cádiz on May 9, 1502. Because he felt too ill to act as captain, my father had asked his good friend, Diego Tristán of Castile, to take command. "It's good to be here at last," the Admiral said to me. "I can never be truly happy on land." He turned to the captain. "Let us make haste to be off." Captain Tristán shouted orders, red-capped sailors cast lines every which way, and we were in motion, the white walls of Cádiz shrinking behind us. My father smiled broadly, and the wind cracked the sails above us. I could see his spirits were high as he stood proudly on the quarterdeck. Feeling the wind at my back, smelling the clean salt air, I was filled with joy as we began our voyage.

We had gone but a short way when suddenly my father swore

his strongest oath. "By San Fernando, the wind is changing," he cried.

I looked at him in surprise, and then at the mainsail, which was fluttering helplessly, no longer bellied out full of wind.

"She's beginning to luff," my father said. "We must hold the caravel steady until we can bring her about."

Captain Tristán shouted orders, and the men began to pull on the sails. Clouds now covered the sun, which a moment before had been shining brightly. A drop of rain hit my nose, and a gust of wind nearly tore my cloak off me.

"Now," shouted Captain Tristán through a hatch on the quarterdeck. The men in the steerage below could not see either sails or sky and depended on orders from above. "Pull hard," yelled the captain. "We're heading for the cove. Good, good. Hold the tiller for all you're worth. There, she's changed course. Good work."

Captain Tristán turned to my father. "We shall have to shelter a while at Santa Catalina, Don Christopher." This was the fortress which guarded the harbor at Cádiz.

The Admiral spoke to me. "Here is your first lesson at sea, Fernando. Remember, the weather is no man's slave. We can make no headway against this southwest wind."

"How long will we have to wait, Father?"

"God only knows."

Although the delay was frustrating, I took advantage of it to become acquainted with our ship, from the depths of the hold, where the wine was stored in casks set upon the ballast stones, to the crow's nest at the top of the foremast—though this last was not my idea.

"Let me see what kind of a head you have, Fernando," my

father said to me late on our second day at Santa Catalina. The rain had stopped, but the sky was still gray. "Climb to the crow's nest—there, up that rope ladder."

I stood at the foot of the ladder and looked up the mast. My stomach felt watery, and I closed my eyes. "Up there, Father?"

"Up." His voice told me he meant it, and I began to climb. The rope ladder swayed under me, and I clung to its sides. "Don't look down," I whispered to myself. "Just keep climbing." I tried not to think and kept my gaze on the little platform high above me. I climbed steadily and at last hoisted myself onto the platform, feeling panic rise as my legs dangled over empty space for a moment.

I grabbed the rail around the platform and looked toward the land. Although it was a bit foggy, I could see the waves breaking on shore and white mounds of salt drying out on the flats in the distance. Both land and sea were level, and it was not always clear where one ended and the other began. The other three caravels of our fleet bobbed nearby.

My uncle Bartholomew, the Adelantado, or Governor, of the Indies, was aboard the *Bermuda,* the ship closest to our own. I strained my eyes to see him. Instead I saw two well-dressed men talking to each other—the Porras brothers, no doubt. Francisco de Porras was the captain of the *Bermuda,* and his brother, Diego, was the Crown's representative and chief clerk and auditor. His job was to keep track of the gold we found. I knew that my father had his doubts about the loyalty and competence of the Porrases, which was why he had asked Bartholomew to sail on the *Bermuda.* As we were to discover, my father's foresight proved extremely wise.

The Admiral had no such fears for the other ships. Just behind the *Bermuda* was the *Gallega,* captained by Pedro de Terreros, who had been on all my father's voyages. Juan Quintero, the owner of the *Gallega,* had been the boatswain on the *Pinta* during the first voyage. Last in our little fleet of roundtops was the *Vizcaína*. Bartolomeo Fieschi, an old and trusted friend of the Columbus family in Genoa, was her captain. Like me, Flisco—for so my father called him—was making his first trip across the Ocean Sea.

A gull flew past and squawked as if surprised to see my face so high. I could feel myself swaying with the mast. I had had enough and forced myself to climb down the ladder. I shall never understand why it is so much harder to go down where you wish to be than it is to climb where you have no desire to go.

I stood up straight when I felt the deck beneath my feet, but my legs trembled. If he noticed, my father made no mention of it.

"Good work, Fernando. Should we ever need a lookout, I'll recommend you for the post."

"Father, I pray the lookouts on this voyage stay healthy. I wouldn't want to deprive any sailor of his job."

I looked up at the swaying rigging and felt happy to be back on deck. I knew my father was worried because Captain Tristán had not assigned a lookout to the crow's nest while we were at anchor. It was for lack of a proper lookout that the *Santa María* had run aground and broken into pieces on the first voyage. But if Captain Tristán did not want a lookout for now, that was fine with me!

By the next day the squall had played itself out, and we set sail once more. The Admiral had heard that the Moors were besieging the Portuguese at Arcila on the west coast of Morocco, and ordered Captain Tristán to sail in that direction so that we might lend our small force of arms in their defense.

I was glad to see Santa Catalina grow smaller in the distance, for the sight of that fortress had brought back painful memories of my father's former glory.

In September 1493 my brother Diego and I had stood on those same fortress walls while my father's great fleet of the second voyage to the Indies streamed past us. Then the Admiral had seventeen magnificent vessels and over a thousand men at his command. Their Highnesses had appointed him Admiral of the Ocean Sea and Viceroy and Governor-General of all the mainlands and islands he might discover, ordaining that he keep one-tenth of all the gold, silver, pearls, gems, spices, and other merchandise he might obtain. These rights and privileges were to be passed on to his heirs forever and ever.

I glanced at the three little caravels plowing through the gray sea behind the *Capitana*. Our four ships together carried only one hundred and forty men.

Ah, but in 1493 the whole of Spain lay at my father's feet. Because he had found a new way to the Indies, everyone said Spain would soon rival Portugal as the only other European power with ships sailing to the Orient. Spaniards would colonize Española; Spanish priests would bring the word of our Lord to the Indian peoples; Spanish explorers would fill the royal treasury with gold. No longer would the Arabs have their monopoly on spices from the Orient. The glory of Venice would sink into the sea, while Castile and León ruled triumphant. Or so people said in 1493.

I was only five at the time, but I could still remember the booming of the cannon and the music of the harps and trumpets saluting the fleet as it sailed, united and handsome, past Santa Catalina on out to sea. So many colors were flying that day they became entangled in the rigging. I held tightly to Diego's hand and watched that glorious armada until my eyes ached with pride.

What a difference the years had wrought.

III / *The Admiral of the Mosquitoes*

NOW IT SEEMED all Spain was at my father's throat. I had first learned of this change two years before at the court in Granada. Although I had been a page for several years— I served Prince Juan until his death in 1497, then the Queen—I confess I did not pay any attention to intrigue or the gossip of my elders. When I was not waiting on the Prince or the Queen, I either buried my nose in a book or asked one of the courtiers to tell me tales of romance and chivalry.

Then, one day in the summer of 1500, I saw at close hand what kind of men my father had taken to Española.

Hearing a clamor in one of the patios, I peered around a doorway and saw some fifty men marching about, shouting and waving grapes in the air. Finally they sat down and began to eat the grapes. "This is all we have to eat," they shouted as His Highness,

King Ferdinand, walked by. "We have no money. The Admiral Christopher Columbus has refused to pay us. Pay, pay!"

I could not believe my senses, and I ran to find Diego. When the men saw Diego and me together later on, they called after us, "There go the sons of the Admiral of the Mosquitoes." According to the stories those scoundrels told, that was all they had found in the Indies—mosquitoes. Their brazen uproar went on for days.

One night Diego found me weeping in a corner.

"What's the matter?" he asked, putting his arm around me.

"Those men—I hate them. Why do they speak so rudely of us and our father?"

"You must learn not to pay attention to such shameless wretches, my brother," Diego said. He tousled my hair. "They're coarse, lazy—and liars. You know our father wouldn't cheat anyone. In fact, he's doing everything in his power right now to established a peaceful and productive colony on Española. But those so-called settlers out there want only two things: more gold and more Indian slaves than they're entitled to.

"The settlers who find gold won't turn it over to Father, even though he's supposed to collect it and keep accounts for the Crown. And the ones who don't find gold are bitter and resentful and say that Father is nothing but a foreigner with an empty title and a brand-new coat of arms. He might just as well not be Viceroy for all the respect they show him. Many have openly rebelled against his authority. They refuse to clear the land or to build houses or even to plant the seeds they took to Española. They force the Indians to work until they die of exhaustion, steal food and gold from them as they please, and kidnap the Taino girls and women —they even sell them to one another. The Indians may be slaves, but they are entitled to some Christian justice from us."

"How do you know so much?" I had begun to feel better.

"First, little brother, I'm much older than you, and I understand these things. Second, the Columbus family has friends at court, and they've told me what they've heard. Our father's the greatest navigator the world has ever seen—they all agree on that. But he is not a good administrator, they say, because he's too good a man to see the evil in other men's hearts—or, rather, he's not wise enough to subdue it, even with the help of our uncle Bartholomew, the Adelantado. I know it must hurt you to hear this as it hurt me. But perhaps the rumor is true."

"They lie," I shouted angrily, pulling myself away from Diego.

"They may be mistaken, but perhaps not," Diego answered solemnly.

"What do you mean?" I asked, surprised to hear my brother speak in this way.

"Bobadilla," said Diego.

"What about him?" I had seen Francisco de Bobadilla at the court many times, and I knew that their Highnesses had sent him to Española a few weeks before.

"Bobadilla was dispatched to Española to investigate the reports about our father and the state of the colony."

I was quiet, but my heart lay heavy in my chest. I knew the Queen would not have taken such an action unless she felt something was seriously wrong on Española.

My misgivings proved to be well-founded. Late that fall we received the terrible news: the Admiral had been returned to Seville in chains. Fray Gaspar Gorricio took him in—on charity! —at Las Cuevas monastery in Seville, where he was waiting for permission to travel to Granada. Diego did his best to discover what had happened in Española, but none of the stories made sense to us, though we were sure an injustice had been done our father.

Just before Christmas the Admiral arrived in Granada with

Bartholomew and his other brother, Don Diego, who had been on Española with him. The story he told us was complex in detail but simple in theme: he had been betrayed by Bobadilla.

Bobadilla had arrived on Española to find Don Diego in charge of the capital city of Santo Domingo and my father and Bartholomew gone. Accusing the Admiral and the Adelantado of abandoning their duties, Bobadilla ordered that their property be seized. He even went so far as to move into the Admiral's own house. He had Don Diego arrested and sent for my father. Actually, the Admiral and the Adelantado had gone to another part of the island to quell a rebellion by Spaniards, but Bobadilla refused to listen to my father when he returned, preferring instead to believe the lies he heard from our enemies in the city. They accused my father and uncle of being cruel tyrants and rejoicing in the shedding of Spanish blood. Bobadilla then had my father arrested and thrown into jail, bound in chains. When Bartholomew arrived in Santo Domingo a few days later, Bobadilla had him arrested too. Bobadilla was so eager to demonstrate his power and establish his popularity with the rabble that he pardoned all the rebels and gave them permission to gather as much gold as they could. Then, after a hasty inquest, he sentenced the three Columbus brothers to be tried in Spain.

After an audience with the King and Queen, in which my father explained the injustice of what had happened, their Highnesses eventually pardoned him and his brothers, commanding that his share of the income from the gold found on Española— and his property—be restored. He spent the following summer in Granada with us, where the easeful life and the sun helped to restore his broken health and spirits. But in September he was stricken to the heart to hear that their Highnesses had appointed Don Nicolás de Ovando, Knight Commander of Lares, to be Viceroy of the Indies in the Admiral's place. This meant that my father's right to govern Española was suspended. Little was left him but the Columbus property in Santo Domingo and the income from gold, and he demanded that Bobadilla account for it to an agent. By the time Ovando and the agent sailed for Española in February, my father had returned to the hospitality of Fray Gaspar at Las Cuevas, and it was from there that he wrote to their Highnesses, requesting permission to make the fourth voyage. It was soon after this was granted that he told me I was to go with him.

Shortly before he departed on the High Voyage, he received a letter from their Highnesses, in which they confirmed all their promises.

"All that we have granted you shall be preserved intact according to the privileges that you have received from us. . . . Be assured we shall look after your sons and brothers as is just, and your office shall be vested in your son. But all this can be attended to after you have sailed; we therefore pray you not to delay your departure.

"I THE KING   I THE QUEEN"

When we boarded the *Capitana,* I noticed chains hanging in my father's cabin. He saw me looking at them and said, "Those are the chains in which I returned to Spain, my son. When the time comes for me to leave this vale of tears, see that they are buried with me to remind God of how I have suffered at the hands of men. Our Saviour retains his power and wisdom as of old; above all things He punishes ingratitude."

IV / At the Binnacle

"WHY SO GLOOMY, Fernando? The clouds have blown away from the sky, but there still seems to be a shadow on your face."

My father had come up behind me and stood by my side. I did not want him to know what I had been thinking, and so I answered, "I can no longer see the coast, Father. Spain is out of sight."

"But not out of mind. Homesick already?" He laughed. "Never look back, Fernando. You can't return to what's past; nothing stays the same. You're not the boy you were last week, nor are the people you left behind in Granada the same. You are traveling on a different road now, and you must concentrate on it, always looking forward to what you may discover ahead." He gazed for some moments at the horizon behind us, then turned to me again.

"There's nothing back there for us now. Come, I want you to meet someone."

Together we climbed down the ladder from the quarterdeck to the main deck, and made our way to the steerage at the stern. My father greeted our pilot, Juan Sánchez, a tall man with large eyes and a short, dark beard. "How does it look?" he asked.

"All in good order, Admiral," Sánchez replied. "We should reach Arcila the day after tomorrow if the wind holds."

I looked around the steerage. One of the men was holding on to the tiller, steering the rudder, which projected from the stern. It was Juan Sánchez's duty to give him instructions, I knew.

"Do you want to see how the compass works?" Sánchez asked me.

"I confess it's a mystery how this can help you," I said, pointing to the compass, which seemed to float in a bowl on top of the binnacle.

"Do you see the fleur-de-lis? If we were heading north it would be pointing to this line that goes down the side of the bowl."

"How can a fleur-de-lis painted on a piece of card tell you north?" I was puzzled.

"The fleur-de-lis by itself means nothing. It's the needle on the underside of the card that's important. It's been magnetized by a lodestone, and so it always points north. Since we wish to travel to Morocco, we must head southwest; that is, we set our course in the direction almost opposite to where the fleur-de-lis is."

I must have looked bewildered beyond words at this, for my father and Juan Sánchez both laughed out loud. They ignored me after that, and became engrossed in a conversation full of wests and wests by souths.

All this while I had been aware of a tall, thin boy standing at the binnacle, watching an *ampolleta*. His face was serious, but his dark eyes were friendly.

"Do you know how that thing works?" I asked him, pointing to the compass. "I'm still not sure what the fleur-de-lis has to do with north."

"It's really not hard once you get the hang of it," he said. "Just remember that a magnetized needle always points north, and the fleur-de-lis always points north too because the needle is set directly under it."

I thought I saw what he meant but not entirely. To hide my confusion I pointed to the ampolleta.

"What's that hourglass for?" I asked.

"As soon as the sand reaches the bottom of the glass, I'm supposed to turn it over. That means a half hour has passed. Eight half hours equal four hours, and four hours is the length of each watch—except for the dog watches, of course."

"Of course," I repeated. I did my best to sound knowledgeable, but by now I was thoroughly mystified. What was a dog watch? I thought of the Irish wolfhound my father had brought along on the voyage and imagined him sitting on the poop deck watching—watching what?

"And so that everyone will know when a half hour has passed, I have to sing each time I turn the glass," the boy went on. "By the way, my name is Francisco Flores y al-Khalidi. Everyone calls me Paco. You're the Admiral's son, aren't you?"

I had been away from the court less than a week and already I had lost my manners. I should have asked him his name before he told me.

"That's right. But even so, I must confess I know as little about ships and sails and watches as I do about compasses." Paco nodded at what I said.

"To be honest with you," he said, "I'm new at all this, too. This is my first voyage. I shipped on as a gromet—that's a kind of junior sailor—in Seville two weeks ago, and it's only now that I'm beginning to feel that I'm learning anything." He glanced at the ampolleta. "The glass is almost empty. I'll have to sing soon."

I watched as the last grains of sand hit bottom. Paco turned the ampolleta over and began to sing.

> *"One hour has passed, another is going.*
> *If so my God wills, more will fly past.*
> *Let's pray to my God for a good voyage,*
> *May His Blessed Mother keep us safe from the tempest."*

Paco's voice rang high and pure over the creaking of the ship and the shouts of the sailors. My father and Sánchez stopped their talk to listen. When Paco finished, my father spoke to him.

"Fray Gaspar was right. You sing very well, young man."

Paco bowed his head as my father was speaking. "Thank you, my Admiral. It pleases me to know I have pleased you."

My father turned to me. "This is the person I wished you to meet," he said. "Fray Gaspar at Las Cuevas recommended Paco as a sincere young man who needed to learn a trade. I thought he would be a good companion for you, and so I suggested he ship with us. I see you have already met. I'll leave you now, Fernando, in good hands."

Nodding at us both, my father took his leave.

I stayed with Paco at the binnacle long enough to find out that aboard ship the day was divided into periods called watches. Every four hours a new group of men, also called a watch, would replace those who were on duty. I thought it a hard system: four hours work and four hours sleep for each of the two watches. In the afternoon and evening, the watches were further divided into stretches of only two hours each. These were the dog watches, but why they were so called, I have no idea.

Before I knew it, another half hour had passed and Paco had inverted the ampolleta and begun his song—a different one this time. I stayed until he had finished singing, then went forward to the bow, where I stood and watched the diamonds dancing on the sea for a long time.

V / Crossing the Ocean Sea

WE HAD HEARD that the Portuguese were in dire straits, but by the time we arrived in Arcila, on May 13, the Moors had lifted their siege and departed. My uncle Bartholomew and I went ashore on a courtesy visit while my father remained aboard the *Capitana* to entertain some cousins of his late wife—Diego's mother—Dona Felipa Moniz, who had been Portuguese. Though we did nothing for the people at Arcila, they were grateful for our offer of assistance and wished us a prosperous voyage. Later that night we set sail for the Canary Islands, which was to be our last stop on this side of the Ocean Sea.

Our sojourn in the Canaries was uneventful. We took on water and firewood, and finally, on the night of May 25, the *Capitana*, the *Vizcaína*, the *Gallega*, and the *Bermuda* set off, west by south, to catch the trade winds. As my father had found out on his earlier voyages, if the trades are at your back, you simply let them push you across the sea.

The excitement of being under way at last kept me from sleeping that first night out on the Ocean Sea. It seemed to me I stood for hours wondering what lay ahead of us, and gazing at the water slapping past our bow. When the eleven o'clock watch came on duty, I curled up in my cloak on the deck. I had never seen so many stars as in that sky above me. I felt as if I had left this poor world and were on my way to Heaven.

At last I fell asleep, lulled by the confident sweep of the *Capitana* through the deep water. I did not hear the three o'clock watch come on duty. The next thing I remember was seeing the sails change from gray to gold as the sun came up over the open sea.

The new morning was fresh and cool, and the dawn watch began to scrub the decks with sea water, as they did every day before being relieved by the next watch. I grabbed a quick breakfast. Munching a few cloves of garlic, I poured some olive oil on a biscuit—baked in Spain and still clean and fresh. Then I helped myself to some sardines, and went to sit with the men who were coming on for the seven-to-eleven watch.

"At the rate we're going, this flying pig will reach the Indies in three days," boasted Juan Sánchez.

"We'll be lucky if this wooden nag makes it across at all," retorted Master Bernal, our apothecary and surgeon.

"Hey, man, don't worry," said Juan de Noya, the cooper. "Our Admiral's the best sailor this world has ever seen. He knows the Ocean Sea better than you know your own wife." With his red stocking cap and easy smile de Noya had a jaunty look. I liked him at once.

Master Bernal was not amused. "Lucky, that's what the Admiral is. I hope his luck and God's will are in agreement. I want my share of that gold he keeps saying is out there."

The conversation was beginning to make me squirm. I didn't

know what to say. Fortunately, one of the sailors, Gonzalo Díaz, broke it up by saying with a laugh, "Pardon me, friends. I can't worry about gold now. Nature is calling me to the *jardines*. Out of my way." He stood up and headed for the side of the caravel. The jardines, or gardens, were wooden seats slung over the rail, where all, from Admiral to gromet, answered the calls of nature. Nothing is private on a ship.

De Noya raised his heavy brows, which almost met over his nose, and signaled to me. "Señorito, I'm going below to check the casks. Would you care to accompany me?"

I stood up gladly.

The hold was dark and smelled sour. All the runoff from the decks washed down into the bilge, and the foul water sloshed over the ballast stones, keeping the rats alert. I looked around but did not see any in the column of light that fell through the open hatch.

"That Bernal is an unhappy man," de Noya said to me. "It's too beautiful a morning to waste in a stupid argument with him. Not that it's so beautiful down here." He laughed.

De Noya's laughter made me feel cheerful enough to try a quip of my own. "I don't smell any orange blossoms," I said.

"Nor do I," said de Noya, smiling as he bent down to examine a cask. "These humble casks have an interesting history, señorito. The Arabs have used them for centuries, but it wasn't until Vasco da Gama sailed around the Cape of Good Hope that a European ship took advantage of them for storing wine and water below the deck. I've got to keep my eye on them to be sure they're not leaking."

His inspection over, de Noya thumped the last cask and said, "Ah, these are in good shape yet." He straightened up as much as he could without hitting his head on the low deck above.

"What are those corded things hanging from the beams?" I asked. "Fishnets?"

"No, no. Haven't you ever seen hammocks before? They're woven by the people of the Indies, who use them for sleeping. Way back in 1493, when your father first saw them, he decided to get some for the comfort of his sailors. Before that everybody slept on the deck."

"That's where I slept last night."

"Well, it's all right in good weather, but how would you like it in the rain?"

"Then I'd sleep in the officers' cabin; that's what I did when we were off Santa Catalina."

"Spoken like an admiral's son. But suppose you were just a sailor or a gromet?"

"It's hard for many, I guess," I conceded.

"At least now the men can sleep down here in bad weather— if they don't mind the smell."

"And the cockroaches," I said, fascinated by the swarms of insects scurrying about on the casks. There wasn't enough room for them all, and they kept falling off onto the ballast stones below.

"And the rats. Well, let's not spend any more time down here than we have to. It's too crowded."

We climbed to the deck and de Noya slammed the hatch shut. "I'd like to take a nap on that right now," he sighed, pointing to the hatch cover. It was the favorite sleeping place of the sailors because it was the only flat surface on the main deck, which was curved so that the water could run off.

At eleven, when the next watch came on, we had a hot meal, cooked on the galley fire on the deck in front of the forecastle.

My father always took his meals alone in his cabin. Sometimes I joined him, but today I felt like eating with the crew out of the common bowl. Master Bernal was not around, for which I was thankful.

As we ate the stew made from some kind of stringy salt meat —I think it was horse—the men sighed and talked about the tender lamb from Cordova and the succulent pork from Estremadura. Despite all the sighing, by the time they had finished eating, every bone thrown on the deck had been picked so clean it shone.

I said nothing to the crew about the aristocratic food I was used to at court. But though I kept quiet, I too longed for the delicacies I knew, especially the sweet oranges, juicy pomegranates, and fresh dates. At that moment I would have given all the gold in India for a bunch of white grapes from Guadalajara. I sighed and thought about how all sailors must long for the good things they leave behind.

I consoled myself by thinking about what we did have on board. We were lucky, for my father had written a letter to the Catholic Sovereigns about what he thought a proper shipboard diet should be, and we had it all. He had explained to me that these foods store well and were very like what the peasants eat on land. We had good biscuit, salted flour (from which—like Arab seamen— we could bake unleavened bread in the ashes of our galley fire), wine, salt meat, oil, vinegar, cheese, chickpeas, lentils, beans, salt fish—and fishing tackle—honey, rice, almonds, and raisins. In spite of the grumbling, we were eating well.

There is no doubt that de Noya looked contented when he curled up for his siesta on the hatch, his red cap pulled down over his eyes.

VI / *"A Little Wax Candle, Rising & Falling"*

T THREE O'CLOCK in the afternoon, when the first
dog watch began, there was usually time for talking.
Their red caps tossed aside, the men would sit around barefoot on
the deck and spin yarns, or when the sea was especially calm,
jump overboard and go for swims. I was too frightened to do
this—suppose the caravels left me behind?—and would content
myself with pouring buckets of sea water over myself, then drying
in the sun. Often Paco and I would take turns splashing each
other.

We were several days out from the Canaries when we began
to see the weed. It floated on top of the ocean in every direction,
and the caravels plowed through it without hindrance. I recalled
that in Granada my uncle Don Diego had told me about this
strange phenomenon, but when Paco asked me about it, all I

could remember was that Uncle Diego said it went on for leagues and leagues.

"Where does it come from?" asked Paco. "I don't like the way it goes on and on. There are probably monsters lurking in it."

"There's nothing to be afraid of, Paco," I said. "It's just sea-weed. My uncle said it's harmless."

"Well, I'm not going to take any more baths until we're past it. Who knows what creatures we may raise in the buckets?"

I was surprised at Paco's fears of the weed, but, truth to tell, I didn't like the looks of it either. I decided there was only one thing to do, and the next afternoon when my father awakened from his siesta, I asked him to tell me what he knew about the weed. "You saw it on your first voyage, didn't you, Father?"

He leaned back in his chair and yawned. I was sitting tailor fashion on his bunk, eager to have him begin. I loved to hear my father tell stories: he was like an actor who made a tale come alive with gestures and grimaces.

"Well, since it's the weed you want to hear about, I'll begin in the middle," he said. "We were about where we are now—some twelve hundred miles from the Canaries—though I had told the crew we had sailed less so that they wouldn't be dismayed if the voyage should prove long."

"You mean you lied, Father?"

"Of course not. I just wanted the crew to remain calm—remember, no ship had ever come this far west before, and it wasn't easy to convince the men that we were safe. I simply bent the truth a little for all our sakes.

"Where was I? Oh, yes"—he looked at me sternly—"the weather had been as pleasant as Andalusia in April for those twelve hundred miles. Then all at once we began to meet with large patches of weeds—very green as you yourself have seen.

They looked as though they had recently been washed away from the land. The men began telling each other that we were near some island. I wanted to put a halt to their guesswork, so I told them, 'Perhaps we are near an island but not a continent. The continent lies farther ahead.' "

"How could you be so sure of that, Father?" I asked.

"When I lived in the Canaries—years before you were born— I had an old friend, Pepe, a redoubtable fisherman, who had once sailed out to sea and gotten lost for quite a while in the same weed we see now, Fernando. That old sea dog told me of his adventure —he was lucky enough to have made it back home—and advised me not to be fooled. 'That weed goes on forever,' he said. 'Every minute I expected to be cast upon some island, but never an island did I see, just that infernal, eternal weed.' I remembered old Pepe's story and continued to urge the crew to be patient.

"But the next day, we saw even more weed. 'Surely it comes from some river nearby,' the men cried." His arms apart and elbows bent, my father gestured with his hands in broad mimicry of the baffled sailors. I laughed as he went on with his story.

"One of the sailors reached into the sea with a gaff hook and hauled some weed aboard. Clinging to a frond there was"—the Admiral leaned toward me and took my hand—"a crab as small as your thumbnail." He pinched my thumb, sat back, and laughed. "The sailors took this little beast of a crab to be a great omen." My father's voice grew deeper. " 'Surely we are near land,' they insisted."

He continued in his normal voice. "I urged them to have faith in me and not believe in little crabs. Later some pelicans came aboard—another sign, usually, of the neighborhood of land—and we continued to see large quantities of the weed for the remainder of that week. One morning there was so much floating toward us from the west that the ocean seemed to be covered with it. On that day we saw a whale and more sea birds."

"What kinds of birds, Father?"

"Oh, more pelicans, a turtledove, gulls, terns, frigate birds, boatswain birds, birds I had never seen before. Some were undoubtedly land birds, and I began to wonder myself if we weren't near some island.

"The sailors, as you can imagine, began to grow alarmed as day after day they witnessed signs of land but no land itself. Then, while the wind kept blowing us steadily westward across the glassy sea, they grew afraid. They murmured that the wind would never blow them back to Spain, only endlessly westward.

"But then, Fernando," my father continued, leaning forward in his chair, "something mysterious happened. The sea rose all by itself into a great wave, astonishing every one of us. Moments later I realized that the rising of the sea was an omen to remind me of Moses, who had commanded the sea to part when he led the Jews from Egypt." He leaned back in his chair with a smile of satisfaction. "It was a clear sign that God was with me.

"I reassured the crew with this knowledge, and then, a few days later—it was the twenty-fifth of September—Martín Alonzo Pinzón, captain of the *Pinta,* called out with great joy, 'Land! I see land!' We fell on our knees and gave thanks to God. But after sailing all night and most of the next day, we discovered that what we had thought was land was nothing but clouds.

"Had the crew known how far we had actually traveled, their patience would have been strained to the limit. As it was, they swallowed their disappointment, and we continued sailing on a sea that was like a river, flowing steadily westward. By now I suspected that it wouldn't be long before we reached Cipangu."

The Admiral got up from his chair and rummaged through

his writing table. Picking up a parchment scroll, he came and sat down on the bunk next to me. He unrolled the parchment and said, "Look at this map, Fernando. Here is Europe, and way over here to the left is Cathay—we know this because of Marco Polo. Now, he has written that Cipangu—he never saw it, mind you, but he had reliable information—is fifteen hundred miles east of Cathay. We all know today that the world is round, but many learned men think the Ocean Sea is much wider than I say it is. When I was a young man working in Lisbon with Bartholomew, I calculated that the distance between Spain and Cathay was less than four thousand miles—and my first voyage showed I was right. Cipangu is only about twenty-four hundred miles west of Spain."

The Admiral returned to his chair, leaving the map to curl back on itself.

"Now, to continue the story. On the night of October 9 we could hear flocks of birds and even saw them against the moon. But by this time the sailors had seen so many false signs of land, so much of that accursed weed, so many birds, so many clouds that looked like islands, that they no longer knew what to believe.

"The next night a group of Galicians and Basques aboard the *Santa María* could stand the suspense no longer. They demanded in no uncertain terms that I turn back.

"I reasoned with those hardheads for all I was worth and cheered them as best as I could, but they would not give in. Finally I had to promise to turn back if we didn't sight land within two or three days. That pacified them for the moment, and they returned to their duties."

"Would you really have turned back, Father?"

"No, but it was expedient to let them believe I would," he said with a sly grin. "The next day, as we steered west southwest through heavy seas, the crew of the *Pinta* picked up a stick from the water. It looked as if it had been carved with an iron tool. Then they found a board, a piece of cane—"

"A piece of what?" I interrupted.

"A plant that grows on land," he answered. "Next, the crew of the *Niña* saw a stalk loaded with roseberries and other signs of land. These encouraged the men, and they grew cheerful, for this time I told them there could be no doubt that land was near.

"Then, at ten o'clock that night—it was October 11—I saw a light at sea. It was so uncertain a thing—like a little wax candle, rising and falling—I wasn't sure whether to call it land. I pointed it out to Rodrigo Sánchez, the Queen's comptroller, but he couldn't see it. 'Land is near,' I told the crew. 'To the first man who sights it I will give a silken jacket in addition to the Crown's reward.'

"Our three ships sped on, silver in the moonlight." My father leaned forward, spreading out his arms. "At last we saw a white sand cliff shining under the moon. Then another, with a dark line connecting the two.

" *'Tierra! Tierra!'* shouted Rodrigo de Triana, the lookout aboard the *Pinta.* I crossed myself and said a silent prayer of thanksgiving.

"We took in our sails and lay to until daybreak. The next morning"—the Admiral leaned back with a smile—"we found we were near a small island called Guanahaní in the Indian language. We went ashore, and our eyes feasted on the sight of trees—very green and laden with fruits—and many streams of water."

"Were there any people?"

"Oh, yes, many. And when I saw how friendly they were, I realized they could be converted to our holy faith much more easily by gentle means than by force. I presented them with some of the red caps the sailors wear, strings of beads, and other trifles. They were delighted."

My father stood up and stretched. "Well, I could go on, Fernando, but this is the end of the story of how we crossed the Ocean Sea—through the weed—and came upon the Indies."

"It's a wonderful story, Father. Thank you for telling it."

"It was my pleasure. Now, if you will leave me I must work on my calculations while it's still daylight."

I went out on deck and looked over the side of the caravel. We were still plowing through the weed. The sea was very smooth —like a river, just as my father had said. Once again I told myself that I was crossing the Ocean Sea—and this time I believed it.

VII / *A Good & Prosperous Voyage*

ONE DAY MELTED into the next as we sailed before the trade wind, hardly touching the sails, for the wind blew so true. By this time Paco and I were good friends. I had repeated my father's story about crossing the Ocean Sea, and Paco no longer worried about the weed, though he still resisted the idea of bathing in the sea water.

We let down buckets into the sea to try to bring up the weed. Now and then we would find a small crab, which would creep over our hands, while we giggled because it tickled. The sun on the blue sea and the brisk wind made me feel so giddy one afternoon that I began to laugh over nothing. "Paco," I called. "Come here."

He climbed out of the ship's boat, where he had been sitting, and came over to me. "What is it?" he asked.

"I don't know," I said. "I just feel happy. Don't you?"

"Ah, señorito, it's been so long since I felt happy that I can't remember what happiness is. The sun is out, the wind is refreshing, yet—"

"Yet you're unhappy. I'm sorry, Paco. Is there anything I can do?"

"It's been like this ever since my mother and father died of the fever. Fray Gaspar at the monastery said that time would heal this wound in my heart, but it's already been two years, and I still feel the pain. Perhaps it was a mistake to leave Seville. At least there I could see my sister, who is a scullery-maid in an inn, from time to time. Here I have no one."

I felt somewhat put out when Paco said that, yet I did not wish to intrude by saying that he had me—perhaps he did not want me as his confidant. Not knowing what to say to make him feel better, I changed the subject.

"Look, there's a frigate bird!" I shouted as a large bird swooped over the deck. "My father showed me one earlier. He says that instead of catching its own food it chases pelicans through the air until they drop their excrement in fright—and then swallows it."

"That can't be!" Paco exclaimed. He looked animated again.

"But it's so," I replied, laughing. "Doesn't it remind you of certain men who in their greed follow others and steal what they have found, whether excrement or gold?"

Paco shook his head and said, "I believe it about men but not about the birds. It's unthinkable."

We walked forward to the forecastle. Ahead we could see dolphins breaking through the water to the west, their curved backs flashing in and out of the sea. Were they, too, headed for Cipangu? As we watched, I began to feel like a coward for not trying to help Paco. Finally, after staring at the dolphins for a while, I felt less shy and said, "You must miss your parents very much."

Paco turned toward me. His eyes filled with tears. "Yes, I do." He flicked away the tears with the back of his hand. "Our family was very poor. Though my father was born a Christian, my mother was a Muslim who converted when she married. Many of our neighbors wouldn't accept her—you know how people can be sometimes. My father was a carpenter—and a good one too—but because of my mother, he didn't get as much work as he deserved. Well, since the world wasn't friendly to my family, we tended to be closer to one another than most people are. That's why it's so hard for me now to be separated from my sister, Caridad. Fray Gaspar knew my mother well, and he told me that she was a good Christian in spite of her birth. He assures me that my mother and father are together in Heaven, and someday we will be reunited. That helps a little, but it's still hard to be so alone."

I listened thoughtfully. I was only five when I was taken from my mother and brought to the court. "I hardly remember my mother," I told Paco, "so I don't miss her now. My father wanted me to be reared at court—and my mother, Beatriz Enríquez de Arana, was a peasant from a village in the hills near Cordova. That's why he never married her, though he did look after her. I miss the Queen more than I do my mother."

"That must be strange—to have a mother yet not really know her," Paco said.

"I didn't really know my father, either," I added. "This is the first time we've spent so much time together. I guess if I'm close to anyone, it's my brother Diego—but he's eight years older, and we're not that close. Most of the time he just bosses me around."

Suddenly I felt sad. I had not thought of it before, but I was almost as much of an orphan as Paco was, perhaps more of one since he at least had known what it was like to have a real family. I looked at Paco and felt that he understood me.

"Poor Fernando," he said, looking at me thoughtfully. For a moment it seemed that he was much older than I was, even though we were the same age. I felt young and unsure of myself, but then I bridled. I did not like being called poor.

"Poor Paco, too," I said firmly.

He nodded. "You're right. We're both poor." He buried his face in his hands. His shoulders were shaking, and he began sobbing loudly. But when I pulled his hands away from his face, I saw that he was laughing. He clapped me on the back and said, "Come on. Let's try our luck at some fishing."

The fish became more plentiful and varied as we sailed westward. Flying fish—which I had never seen before—would occasionally land on the deck—and end up in the stewpot on the galley fire. One day we saw a whale to the south of us, and another time we harpooned a tuna as big as a man. All forty of us feasted on it.

Juan Sánchez finally succeeded in teaching me how to box a compass, that is, recite all the compass points in order. Thanks to Juan de Noya I could spot a leaking barrel in the hold even in the dark. And I learned something from Master Bernal, too—how to remove a fishhook from my thumb. I even got to enjoy climbing to the crow's nest to watch the sunsets with Paco or Gonzalo Díaz.

But the times I enjoyed most were the evening prayers. As the water slapped the sides of the caravel and the wind cracked the sails above, the men would step softly as they gathered at the stern of the caravel, their red caps in their hands.

One of the gromets—maybe Paco—would trim the binnacle lamp and carry it along the deck, singing:

"Amen and God give us a good night and good sailing.
May the ship make a good passage,
Sir captain and master and good company."

The gromets would lead us in the evening prayers: the Pater Noster, the Ave Maria, and the Credo. Then we would sing, our voices floating over the water: *"Salve Regina, mater miseri-cordia ..."*

The galley fire would be put out, the ampolleta turned over, and the gromet on duty would sing his song, as he would every half hour throughout the night. And we would sail on under the moon, dreaming of tomorrow.

VIII / *The Caribees*

ON THE MORNING of June 15, three weeks after we
had sailed from the Canaries, we arrived at the island of
Matininó. There was a rough sea and heavy wind when I first saw
the Indies, but Matininó was a pretty enough island with green
hills sharply etched against the sky.

Although it was far from grand, it served its purpose. Our
supplies were depleted, so we anchored and stayed long enough
to gather firewood and take on water from a river. My father
made the men wash their clothes, since there was never enough
water aboard ship to do laundry during the voyage. Paco and I
enjoyed a long freshwater swim in the river; it felt wonderful to
be clean again. As we stood drying in the sun my uncle Bartholomew came up and wrapped me in a bear hug. "Well, Fernando,"
he said, "do you have any idea where you are?"

"Not exactly," I said. "Somewhere in the Indies."

"We may be on Feminea, the island of the Amazons," he said. "Your father and I have never been on this particular island before, but according to what we heard from the Taino on Española, this could well be Feminea."

"You mean the place in the Indian Ocean Marco Polo has written about?" Excited, I turned to Paco. "Did you hear that?"

"What's the island of Feminea?" Paco asked my uncle.

"Surely everyone has heard of the Greek legend of the Amazons?" he said with a wink. I nodded. There had been a copy of Marco Polo's book at the palace in Granada, and I had spent hours reading it. Paco looked puzzled and shook his head.

"Well," my uncle began, "according to Marco Polo—who heard this story from reliable people—the island of Feminea is inhabited solely by women. Once a year the men from the nearby island of Masculina visit it. The women let the men stay for three months and then send them packing, along with all the boys old enough to leave."

"You're telling us a tall story, Uncle," I said. I found some of Marco Polo's tales hard to believe.

"No, no," he insisted. "It's the truth. Your father heard the very same story from the Indians who live on some of the islands around here. They said that Matininó was the island of women. If this is the case, we have more proof that we're in the Indies."

Paco and I looked at each other. Then we surveyed as much of the island as we could see. It was deserted. But if there were Amazons here, what would they do to us?

A short while later Paco and I went back aboard the *Capitana*. We were not afraid, of course, but we felt safer aboard the caravel, and we were both relieved to be under way once more.

When Matininó was well behind us, Paco and I approached my father.

"Uncle Bartholomew says we were on the island of the Amazons. Is that true?"

My father looked thoughtful. "I don't know. We can't be sure, since we saw no one. But perhaps the women don't wish to meet strangers. Let me tell you, though, what happened to us in 1496 on my third voyage.

"Just to the north of Matininó is the island of Santa María de Guadalupe. It's a beautiful island, hilly, covered with trees and waterfalls. We anchored there once, and I decided to take a boat ashore. Suddenly, to my great surprise, a crowd of women rushed out of the woods and let fly a flock of arrows at us. We managed to quiet them down and told them we had come in search of supplies—food, water, wood. They directed us to ask their husbands, who were in the northern part of the island. This led me to think that Santa María de Guadalupe was once the home of the Amazons, since the men and women seemed to live apart.

"But I'm not sure, because on my second voyage we had landed on another part of the island. I sent a company of ten men to scout for supplies, and though we waited and waited, they didn't return. Finally I sent out two hundred men divided into four search parties to look for them.

"It appeared that the inhabitants of the island had no desire whatever to meet with the Spaniards, for as the search parties advanced over the island the people fled from them.

"Finally the searchers came to a village. And do you know what they found there? It makes me sick even to talk about it. They found pieces of human flesh, bones, and even worse, castrated boys from other islands who were being fattened and girls who told us they were being used to produce babies for food."

"You mean we're in the Caribbees?" The awful realization hit me. "Cannibal country?" Now I was happier than ever that we had come across no one on Matininó.

"Correct. You see, there's very little meat on these islands— some birds and some edible rodents and lizards. The Caribs have found another source: people. That's why all the Indians in this part of the world are afraid of the Caribs."

"But what happened to the ten men?" Paco asked. His face was pale.

"Well, when the search party brought those poor boys and girls they had rescued back to the ship, we were more concerned about our men than ever. But as it turned out, they had simply lost their way in the woods. We found them soon enough, so all ended well. Before we left that terrible island—I tell you I saw with my own eyes human skulls lying on the beach—we destroyed all the Caribs' canoes so that they couldn't raid the other islands—at least for a while."

Paco and I looked at each other, then up at the sails. A stiff wind was pushing us away from the dreadful Caribees, and I, for one, was grateful. What kind of a world had we come to?

IX / *Santo Domingo*

WE SAILED ALONG the Caribee islands until we reached the south side of the island of San Juan Bautista, which was much larger than any of the others we had passed. We did not stop there but pressed on to reach Santo Domingo on Española.

My uncle and father had had time to talk on Matininó, and Bartholomew had told the Admiral that the *Bermuda* was a cranky vessel. From the beginning my father had felt that she was not a good ship for exploring shallow waters. According to Bartholomew, she had turned out to be even worse than the Admiral had feared. Not only was she slow, but every time she loaded her sails, one of her sides nearly disappeared under the water. She had caused so much trouble to my uncle during the crossing that my father had decided to stop at Santo Domingo to trade her for another vessel.

I did not know this at the time, but at the urging of Bobadilla, the Queen had told my father that he was not under any circumstances to land at Santo Domingo on his way to India. She was afraid his presence on the island would cause unrest among the Spaniards there, and also, being of good heart, she wanted to spare him the pain of seeing what had happened to his former colony. Although she had told him he might land there on his way back to Spain, in truth she hoped that he would sail around the world and return by way of India and miss Española altogether. My father had agreed to the Queen's restriction because he too was certain he would find the passage to India, and it was a small sacrifice to make in return for being allowed to make the High Voyage at all.

Nevertheless, when we arrived in the harbor of Santo Domingo on June 29, my father sent Captain Terreros of the *Gallega* to the Viceroy, Don Nicolás de Ovando, to request permission to land.

Paco and I couldn't wait to get ashore. Although Santo Domingo wasn't much of a city by Spanish standards—from the caravel we could see that the buildings were only made of wood and thatch—it was relatively civilized for that part of the world, and it would be good to be among our compatriots for a while.

My father had some letters he wished to mail, and of course he wanted to try to trade off the *Bermuda,* but there was an even more urgent reason for disobeying the Queen and stopping in this haven. As we watched Terreros's boat heading for shore, he said to me, "My joints are paining me, Fernando. It's not a good omen."

"What do you mean?" I asked.

"Whenever my rheumatism flares up like this it means we're in for a storm. This is going to be a bad one, the kind the people of the Indies call *uracán.*" His eyes scanned the horizon. The sea looked calm to me. What was he talking about?

"Look how smooth and oily the sea is," he said. "Do you see

those great swells rolling in from the southeast, and how high the tide is? Doesn't the air feel heavy to you? These are the signs of a hurricane," he went on. "I know them well; I suffered through two of them in the past."

I began to feel anxious. More than ever I wanted to be on terra firma.

But it was not to be. A few hours later Terreros returned to the caravel—with bad news. The Viceroy had refused to give us permission to land.

"What happened?" my father asked Terreros. "Didn't you tell him my fears about the hurricane?"

"Of course," said Terreros. "But he just laughed at me. He told me you were some kind of self-styled prophet and soothsayer and spoke to me about you so insolently that I wanted to knock him down. 'What's this nonsense about a storm?' he said. 'Didn't you see that beautiful red sunset and the dolphins and seals on the surface of the sea? Hurricane, indeed. Look, Terreros, do you see that fleet? It's led by Bobadilla, who's getting ready to sail back to Spain with gold for their Majesties. Would he be planning to sail if a storm were brewing?' And then Ovando got on his high horse and said, 'Please, sir, be so good as not to annoy me with tales from the Admiral.'" Terreros looked agitated as he repeated the Viceroy's words.

"So that's Bobadilla's fleet," my father said softly. "I count twenty-eight ships, and I want only one in exchange for the *Bermuda.*" He stood silently for a moment and then said, "It will be a disaster if they sail."

"That's what I told Ovando," said Terreros. "I said you feared a storm, and then I begged him again for refuge—it's only right, according to the laws of the sea. 'Ridiculous,' said Ovando. 'Your Admiral seeks by this ruse to gain the shore that the Queen herself has forbidden him. I won't allow him to land. And why should I stop Bobadilla? Does your Admiral have some plan to avenge himself on that noble servant of the Crown? Bobadilla will sail when he chooses.' That's how that wretch spoke to me, Admiral. I tell you every word he said. I would boil him in oil if I could."

"Your news grieves me deeply, Pedro," my father said. His shoulders drooped as he stood at the rail, looking at the city he had named after his father, its doors shut against him. Then he straightened and said, "There's nothing for it. We must head out to sea and find shelter. The wind is coming from the north, and I fear for our safety in this exposed harbor. Return to your ship, good Pedro, and let's leave this inhuman place."

My father turned, and seeing Paco and me standing there with long faces, said, "You're not so sorry as I am. Fetch Captain Tristán."

We scurried to the steerage and told Tristán my father wished to see him. "Are we to land?" asked Tristán.

I looked around at the men in the steerage; all of them were eager to hear my answer. "Ovando forbids it," I said.

Tristán nodded and left. The men began to grumble. I could feel their hostility, but I stood where I was.

"What about our shore leave?" asked one of the sailors. "Your father promised us a week's rest here."

Master Bernal looked at me coldly. "Your father may have fewer friends than he thinks," he said. I stared at him in surprise. What did he mean?

Juan de Noya came up and clapped his hand on my shoulder. "Ah, don't worry, señorito. We're all disappointed, but it can't be helped."

At that moment Captain Tristán returned and began issuing orders. "Set the course due west. We must find a lee shore if we're to ride out the coming storm."

Silently the men went to work in the heavy air.

X / *Hurricane!*

THE NEXT DAY we rode quietly at anchor close under
the land somewhere to the west of Santo Domingo. The men
were as sullen as the weather, which lay over us like a pall until
the next afternoon. The heavy air, the silence, and the palm trees
standing still as columns on the windless shore made me feel as
if we were trapped in some forgotten corner of the universe where
time had stopped.

And then, without warning, shrieking through the rigging like
a tormented soul, the wind swept down on us. Rain fell, wrapping
great sheets of water around us under the blackest sky I had ever
seen. Whipped and tossed by the waves piling one after the other
onto the deck, the *Capitana* pulled at her anchor cables as if to
defy my father, who had ordered every piece of iron on the caravel
hung onto them. I clung to the rail, praying the cables would not
give before the tempest was over.

All through that terrible night my father called on God and cursed Viceroy Ovando. The wind blew snatches of his speech to my ears, and I heard him speak in despair. "What man ever born of woman could be so heartless as to forbid us the land that I, by God's will and sweating blood, have won for Spain?" I had never before and have never since heard my father speak so angrily, calling Ovando the devil's servant and much worse as we were thrown about like some evil giant's plaything.

I began to wonder if God could even hear our prayers. The fiendish wind and rain, which seemed flung from the bowels of Hell itself, drowned our words as surely as they drenched our bodies. The wind was so strong that, as we found out later, it crushed the entire city of Santo Domingo flat, as if by a giant fist.

By the next morning the wind had lessened, and the rain fell softly: the hurricane was over. By some miracle the anchor cables had held through the night. We fell on our knees on the wrack-strewn deck and gave thanks to God, humbly and with a great feeling of awe in our hearts at the sight of the uprooted trees on the shore.

"They're gone!" I heard my father shout, and for the first time I thought about the other three caravels. I staggered to the rail and frantically scanned the sea. There was no sign of them, not even a plank.

My heart was heavy as we put our ship to rights. We were too exhausted to do more. The next day we sailed west along the coast to the small harbor of Azua, where my father and his captains had agreed to rendezvous if the storm separated them. Would we meet again on this earth?

But all glory to God—the three missing ships were there to greet us in the pretty harbor of Azua.

Tears were running down my face as I watched Bartholomew and my father embrace once we were all on shore. Then my uncle gave me such a hug I thought my ribs would crack. We began to laugh as if nothing had happened. Our comrades Flisco from the *Vizcaína* and Terreros from the *Gallega* ran up to us, and the laughing and hugging began all over again. Little by little we pieced together the stories of our adventures in the hurricane.

"The *Bermuda* ran out to sea as if she were flying under the wind," said Bartholomew. "All night long water washed over that wooden pig's deck, while I cursed Ovando for not letting us go ashore long enough to trade her off."

"What about the Porras brothers?" my father asked.

"They did nothing but scream to heaven while I did my utmost to control that tub." My uncle's voice was full of scorn at their cowardice.

"I've never felt such winds in my life, Christopher," added Flisco. "Thanks be to God that we're all alive."

"I think my men had the worst time of it," said Captain Terreros. "They tried to save the ship's boat—the one I used to go ashore in—by hanging over the stern and dragging it with cables until their arms were almost pulled out of their sockets. The boat was so swamped that the men were finally forced to cut it loose or go under the waves themselves."

Some of the Admiral's enemies later claimed that we survived the hurricane because of my father's magic. If that is so, then magic is the name for the Admiral's genius as a seaman. For we found out later that when Bobadilla's ships had reached the eastern end of Española—he had sailed in spite of my father's warning— the storm hit the fleet with such fury that the flagship carrying Bobadilla went straight to the bottom of the sea with him. In all, over five hundred men lost their lives, and only one of the ships, the *Aguja,* reached Spain; the few others that were spared limped back to Santo Domingo. The largest nugget of gold yet found in the Indies—as big as a melon and weighing almost four thousand pesos—was lost in the storm too, as were the thousands and thousands of pesos' worth of gold aboard Bobadilla's ship.

When I learned this, I could not help but feel that Divine Providence had made Ovando close his eyes and mind to the Admiral's advice. I wondered, too, whether Divine Providence had caused Viceroy Ovando to put the Columbus family's share of gold—four thousand pesos' worth—aboard the *Aguja* with our agent. Everyone said later that the only reason Ovando chose the *Aguja* to carry my family's gold was because she was the worst ship in the fleet. I can't help thinking that God Himself saw that brave little vessel safely to Spain, where my uncle Don Diego received the gold with pleasure. Only in Heaven, it appears, is there justice.

We stayed in the harbor of Azua over a week, repairing the ships and resting after our ordeal. The caulkers and carpenters were busy, but Paco and I had little to do but amuse ourselves. We fished constantly from the deck of the *Capitana* and caught many remarkable kinds of fish. One day, while we were fishing and munching some biscuits, we heard a cry from the *Vizcaína's* ship's boat floating nearby.

We looked up and saw that the men in the boat had spotted a fish shaped like a triangle with a spiny tail—a giant ray—sleeping on the surface of the sea. I was so startled at the sight of that monster—it was as big as a bed—that I dropped my biscuit on the deck. Paco picked it up, kissed it, and gave it back to me. By this time the men had harpooned the ray and tied it to their boat with a long, thick rope so that it would not escape.

All of a sudden the great ray began to swim mightily, dragging the boat across the harbor the way a child pulls a toy. The men in the boat shouted as the ray surged on, hauling them swift and straight as an arrow. Our mouths hung open, the biscuits forgotten, while we watched the boat skim across the harbor with no one working the oars. Eventually the fish grew weak and died, and with much joking and laughing the men on the *Vizcaína* hauled it aboard.

Paco and I looked at each other. Both of us had the same idea. "Do you suppose we could train that fish to pull us across the Ocean Sea?" I asked.

"Why not?" said Paco. "We could harness rays like horses and ride in grand style."

"Even Marco Polo never heard of such a thing," I said.

"For that matter," Paco went on, "why not harness birds to carry us to the moon?"

"Do you really want to go to the moon?" I asked.

"Not yet," said Paco. "Not yet. I'd like to finish this voyage first."

On another day the men of the *Capitana* captured a fish called a manatee. We do not know of this fish in Europe. It resembles a calf but is fatter and better-tasting. The manatee lay on the deck, breathing its last, while Paco and I argued about it and Gonzalo Díaz sharpened his knife for the butchering.

"I believe that many kinds of land animals can live in the sea," Paco said.

"They say the manatee eats the grass found along the shore," said Gonzalo Díaz, deftly slitting the manatee's belly with one stroke.

"That proves it's not a fish," said Paco, "but a calf."

"If so," said I, "it's a calf like no other."

Blood pooled on the deck, and flies began to swarm around the carcass. Just then my father came up. After he had taken a good look at the beast, he shook his head in disbelief and began to laugh.

"Gonzalo, don't you recognize this creature?" he said.

Gonzalo Díaz stopped cutting up the animal and looked at my father in puzzlement.

"Don't you remember seeing three of these disporting themselves in the sea on one of our earlier voyages?"

"I remember mermaids, sir."

"That's right. One of the men cried, 'Look, mermaids,' and we all ran to the side to stare. Everyone was shouting, 'Mermaids, mermaids.' But I wondered then if they were indeed mermaids. They were so ugly, and I'd always heard that mermaids were beautiful. And they had whiskers: I'd never heard of that. What a good joke this is on us," he continued. "Here, right in front of us, is one of those ugly mermaids with whiskers."

Gonzalo Díaz looked at my father and then at Paco and me. My father was laughing so hard that Paco and I couldn't resist joining in. At last even Gonzalo began to laugh. Since the manatee was a "mermaid," it no longer mattered whether it was a calf or a fish.

Until that moment I had no idea of how much strain we were still under. Our laughter washed away Ovando and the hurricane, and we felt free to go on once more.

XI / *Terra Firma*

O UR SHIPS REPAIRED and our rest over, we sailed to the harbor of Brazil, where the brazilwood trees grow. Then we ran into a calm, and currents carried us to some small islands near Jamaica. We called these los Pozos, the Pools, because the men found water there simply by digging holes in the sand.

Finally wind and weather were in our favor, and we set sail across the uncharted sea toward the mainland. After several days we came upon yet other islands, a few miles from the mainland, covered with pines. As we later learned, the largest of them was called Guanaja by the people who lived there. I was eager to go ashore, but my father bade me stay on the *Capitana*. Since this was to be our first contact with people who were unknown to us, he preferred to leave the meeting in the hands of Bartholomew, who went ashore with a party of men.

Impatient at not being allowed to leave the ship, I stood at the rail with my father and Paco, straining my eyes to see what was happening. Several Indians had come to greet Bartholomew, and there was much gesticulating. A few of the sailors roamed a short distance away from the main party, and it looked as if they were trading with some other Indians, though my father had strictly forbidden private trading. All gold and other precious things had to be accounted for to the Crown before shares were taken; in addition my father feared that the sailors, if left on their own, would not behave properly with the Indians, which could cause trouble for us all.

But just then I saw something that made me bless the fact that I had remained aboard. Delighted and amazed, we watched as a marvelous canoe approached us from the direction of the mainland. As long as a galley and eight feet wide, the canoe was made from a single hollowed-out tree trunk, like other Indian canoes I have seen since. It carried twenty-five paddlers and many women and children, who sat, surrounded by merchandise, under a palm-leaf awning in the middle of the boat.

Our ship's boat went out to meet the canoe and brought it alongside the *Capitana*. "What good fortune this is," my father muttered. "We can see what this new country has to offer with no toil and at no danger to us."

The sailors and some of the Indians began to bring aboard cargo from the canoe. The Indian men were wearing cotton mantles and sleeveless shirts embroidered with colorful designs, very like those worn by the Moorish women of Granada. They carried copper hatchets and wooden swords with blades made of flint knives that cut like steel. At one point something that looked like brown almonds fell on the deck of the caravel. Quickly the Indians squatted and picked up every single almond as if it had great value. Much later I found out that these were cacao beans.

"I have never seen Indians like these before," my father said to me wonderingly. "These are a people of great wealth, civilization, and industry." The women covered their faces as the Moorish women do, and when a sailor rudely snatched a breechcloth off one of the Indian men, he immediately covered his genitals with his hands. My father ordered that the cloth be returned to the Indian, for such dignified and modest demeanor greatly impressed him.

We gave the Indians some lace points—the bits of brass which tip the laces we use for our clothing—and other trifles in exchange for their cotton and copper. Although my father was accustomed to capturing several Indians to serve as guides and interpreters, this time he took only one, an old man named Yumbé, who seemed to be the leader and the wisest among the people.

Through signs my father indicated that he wished Yumbé to join us so that we might learn the secrets of the land. When he understood, the Indian smiled. He seemed pleased and honored to be asked to accompany us. Again through signs my father asked Yumbé where the canoe had come from. "Maia," Yumbé said, pointing southwest toward the mainland. He repeated the word several times.

"It must be a fine country to have such people in it," my father said to me. "I'd like to explore it, but it lies westward, and we must go east, for that's where I believe we'll find a strait across the mainland to the south sea and the lands of spices."

My father called to Paco. "This is Yumbé, whom we shall name in Spanish Juan Pérez. Be his guide on the ship and try to learn his language."

"Yes, sir," Paco said, bowing his head. I could tell he was surprised and pleased to be entrusted with this task. He took Yumbé by the elbow and led him to a clear space on the deck. They sat down together, and Paco began their lessons by pointing to himself and saying "Paco" over and over, then pointing to Yumbé and repeating the name "Juan Pérez." I left them to their work and went to help the men carry the goods we had obtained to my father's cabin.

Uncle Bartholomew came back from his mission a short while later and told us that his trading had come to naught. He was delighted to hear about the Maian people.

"My story is quite different," he said. "When I showed the Indians I met pearls and grains of gold, they offered to buy them from us! When I kept insisting that I wanted to buy gold and pearls from them, they just shook their heads. Finally they did show us some pieces of earth, but it was only fool's gold." He stopped and gave a laugh. "Some of the sailors thought it was the real thing, though, and bought it. They tried to conceal it from me, but I'd seen what they were up to."

He sighed. "I'm sorry, Christopher, if it displeases you, but I didn't have the heart to punish the men. Diego de Porras gave them a good tongue-lashing, however. He was furious at them for not having told him about the 'gold.' As for me, I felt they'd been punished enough when they found out what their gold was worth."

"I suppose you did the right thing, Bartholomew," my father said. "Still, I don't like the idea of the sailors trying to cheat the Crown. We'll have to keep a better eye on them in the future. At any rate, no harm was done since it's clear there was nothing much to be gained in trading on that island. We'd best be moving again."

By now it was early August, and we soon made terra firma again at Punta Caxinas on the mainland. I learned from one of the sailors that *caxinas* is an Indian word for a tree that bears a fruit resembling wrinkled olives. It has a spongy core which is especially good to eat when cooked.

On Sunday, August 14, my uncle and many of the men from the fleet went ashore a little farther along the lovely, flat, green coast to hear Mass. They went with all banners displayed, though we did not take formal possession of this new land until Wednesday.

On that day more than a hundred Indians dressed like those in the big canoe came bearing food and gifts and watched as we Christians took possession of their land in the name of their Highnesses, the Catholic Sovereigns, Ferdinand and Isabella.

Later, when we were free to roam about, Paco asked me, "Did you notice how the Indians watched us during the ceremony?"

"They seemed very interested in what we were doing," I answered. We had walked down to the edge of the sea, and began to skip stones over the water.

"Do you think they knew we were taking possession of their land?"

"Well, of course they knew. Everybody knows that's how we do it."

"What do you mean, 'everybody knows'? They never saw anything like that before, I'm sure."

"What does it matter if they know or don't know? The point is this land belongs to Spain now, and so do they."

"They certainly don't seem to mind, do they? Or perhaps they don't really understand they belong to Spain now." Paco paused. "It must look odd from their point of view—a group of strangers going through such an elaborate ceremony. I guess that's why they looked so enthralled." Paco dropped his stone. "Look, they're exchanging gifts with your father and the Adelantado." He grabbed me by the elbow and broke into a run. "Let's get closer."

We stopped running when we reached the group that was doing the trading and listened as my father and uncle tried to make the Indians understand that they wanted more food brought for a feast the next day.

I wanted to laugh at all the hand-waving and pointing that was going on; it looked so ridiculous. Many of our ship's people knew something of the language spoken on Española, but Yumbé spoke a tongue that was different not only from that one but also from the speech of the Indians on this part of the coast. When I mentioned this impediment to communication to my father, he shrugged.

"We manage somehow to make ourselves understood, picking up words from each other as we go along. I was concerned about this on my first voyage, so I brought a Jewish convert named Luís de Torres with me. He could speak Hebrew and Arabic as well as Spanish. I thought his command of Arabic—the mother of all languages—would serve me in the Indies, but he was totally useless, since it appears these languages are so different. We live in a world of Babel, Fernando, yet there are always ways in which men can make themselves understood."

It was clear that the Indians were pleased with the gifts we gave them, for the next day over two hundred came down to the shore. This time they brought *chicha,* a bitter wine made from sour corn. I thought it tasted terrible, but our sailors drank their fill and were soon happily drunk. The Indians also brought chickens that were better-tasting than ours, geese, roast fish, and red and white beans.

Although these Indians were polite and generous, it seemed to me they could have no religion. Many of them went about naked except for a cloth over their genitals, though some wore a long sleeveless shirt like ours. Their arms and bodies were tattooed with Moorish-looking designs. Some had lions, others deer, others turreted castles—or so it looked to me—burned into their flesh. For the feast they had painted their faces black and red and drawn stripes of various colors on them. Some had put on beaks like ostriches, and others blackened their eyes. I suppose they did this to appear beautiful, but they looked like demons to me.

But no matter—the food was good and freely given. And if the music from the drums and whistles sounded strange, it lent an air of festivity to the afternoon, as did the chicha. But the sailors who imbibed too freely ended up damning it to the skies the next day as they stumbled about the caravels, their heads bursting with pain.

Since we had come to a region where Yumbé could no longer serve as interpreter, the Admiral gave him some presents and signed that he should return home. Yumbé seemed satisfied with this and remained on shore when we sailed away.

"I'm going to miss him," said Paco as we headed down the coast. "I learned a great deal from him. Do you know what he told me about where we're going?" Paco's eyes glistened.

"What did he say?" I asked eagerly.

"He told me that the Indians down the coast are wild in all respects. And they're black." He paused.

"Black?"

"And they wear no clothes at all. They eat raw fish—and human flesh."

At this point my father joined us and asked, "What else?"

"They pierce holes in their ears big enough to insert eggs." Paco began to laugh. "That Yumbé. His stories are as good as your Marco Polo's any day."

"Indeed they are," my father said softly. "I hope we don't meet up with the people Yumbé described, but let's call the next stretch la Costa de las Orejas—the Coast of the Ears—to remind us to keep our eyes open."

The seriousness in the Admiral's tone stopped Paco's laughter. We looked at each other, bewildered. Would we ever be wise enough to separate truth from fancy on this side of the Ocean Sea?

XII / *Gracias a Dios*

OUR PASSAGE along the Coast of the Ears was un-like anything I had ever known before: one continuous nightmare of never-ending rain, thunder, and lightning.

We encountered no trouble from fierce cannibals with big holes in their ears, only from what my father called no man's slave, the weather. Everything aboard ship was ruined. The sails were torn; rigging, cables, and supplies were lost.

As the wind was strong or weak, we gained or as often lost distance with it when we came about. In a creaking, tedious zig-zag we tacked toward the sea and then were forced back toward the land. So as not to lose the short distance we managed to cover, we were forced to anchor whenever the wind fell slack.

"By San Fernando," my father lamented one evening after twelve days of this, "I swear I've never seen a tempest that lasted so long or was so grim." To make matters worse, the next day he was unable to rise from his bunk. He had succumbed to the chills and fever which plagued many of the men aboard. When he was able to be moved, he was carried to a little house the carpenters had rigged up on the poop deck, and whenever he felt strong enough, he gave orders to men who were by now almost too exhausted to obey them. The rest of the time he slept or tossed about fitfully, while Master Bernal fluttered about him like a stork, applying his leeches and cups to no avail.

I worked hard with the crew day after day, hoping in this way to give the men heart and to comfort my father. Still the tempest raged, no matter how much the men prayed for the weather to change. As they toiled, hauling on the sails or weighing anchors or dropping them, the seamen made vows to be good, to go on pilgrimages once they were safely back in a Christian country again—all the promises people make when they feel the end is at hand. They even listened to one another's confessions. I will not name any names, but before the week was out many strong men had lost their courage and simply sat on the deck unable to move.

Sloshing about on a wet deck, sleeping in soggy clothes, being eaten by infernal mosquitoes, which seemed to know we were too tired to brush them off—I did the best I could. I too prayed for deliverance from this eternal storm, but most of all I beseeched the Blessed Virgin to restore my father's health.

After twenty-eight days of this we had traveled less than two hundred miles.

And then one afternoon as my father stood shakily in front of the little house on the poop deck, we rounded a cape where the coast turned south. The prevailing eastern winds would no longer be against us night and day. "Thanks be to God," said my father.

Relief at our deliverance flooded me, and I echoed his words.

His eyes searched my face as he said, "Let us call this blessed cape Gracias a Dios to remind all who come after us of what we have suffered."

"Amen," I said.

Then my father smiled. "Well, skeleton," he said, "the worst is over."

His words puzzled me. Did I look as haggard as he did? No one in my life had ever called me a skeleton before. I looked down and saw that my baby fat had melted away.

"It's about time, Fernando," said my father, "that you lost the signs of your soft life at court. I'm proud of you. You revived the spirit of the others and acted like a sailor of eighty years. You consoled me, and I see these last weeks have made you a man."

I stood up tall and looked my father in the eye. He was well again. "Thank you," I said quietly. I had no other words to express how I felt.

Although the worst was over, trouble still lay in wait. We had need of wood and water, and on September 16 the four caravels anchored a little farther down the coast at the mouth of a river whose entrance seemed deep and easy.

The Admiral sent the three ships' boats to fetch water, and we watched them disappear behind the thickets of cane growing along the riverbanks.

Abruptly, without warning, the wind freshened, and the sea became heavy, building up a strong surf at the mouth of the river. Two boats came out from behind the cane safely, but then, while we looked on helplessly, disaster struck the third. The heavy surf swamped the boat, which then overturned, and while their companions clung desperately to the boat two men drowned before they could be rescued.

My father named this place the Río de los Desastres to mark our sorrow and gave orders to sail away immediately.

But bad luck does not last forever, and nine days later we found the best country and people that we had yet seen.

XIII / *Cariay*

FROM THE DECK of the caravel Paco and I could see groves of palms, myrobalans, and many other great trees. Parrots of all colors flew through the forest, and red cranes stalked the riverbanks. We were at anchor off a village and region on the mainland named Cariay, as we learned later, not far from an island the Indians called Quiribirí. The island was so high, beautiful, and green that the Admiral named it la Huerta, the Orchard.

"Are we going ashore, Father?" I asked. I wanted to feel solid ground under my feet again. I had had enough of the caravel for a while.

The Admiral stood staring at the mainland. "Wait," he said, patting my hand. "Let's see if the people here are as welcoming as the land."

"Do you expect trouble, sir?" asked Paco.

"One never knows," he answered. "Be patient, and we'll learn what we need to know before we take any rash steps. It is wise to be prudent in strange lands."

I looked around at the other caravels, which had begun to list as the men aboard them crowded to the shoreside rails to look at the beach. I could sense a mixture of eagerness and apprehension on the part of the sailors.

Suddenly a band of Indians came running out of the forest on the mainland and down to the beach, waving bows and arrows and clubs and spears made of palm wood tipped with fishbones. But when they saw that we did nothing to threaten them, the Indians must have realized that we came in peace, for some of them swam out to the ships, offering goods for trade.

"We won't trade yet," the Admiral told us. "If they see we're not eager, they'll bring more goods. I want to know if they have gold, and only if we hold off will we find out."

When several Indians clambered aboard the caravel, my father smiled and held his arms open wide to show that he had nothing to hide. The men, whom we found out were known as the Talamanca people, wore their hair braided around their heads. They offered my father cotton cloaks and shirts, but he shook his head. One Indian took off the pendant he wore around his neck and held it out to the Admiral. He shook his head again, for he could see it was made of *guanín,* a mixture of copper and gold, and this meant that gold was scarce in this country.

I could tell from the Indians' expressions that they were puzzled at my father's refusal of their offerings. As they waited, confused, the Admiral made a sign to Gonzalo Díaz, who came up laden with beads, lace points, and the little jingling bells hawks wear. My father took these things from Díaz and presented them to the Talamanca, making signs that they should accept them and depart, leaving nothing in return. This the Indians did, still looking bewildered.

On reaching the shore, they held up their cloaks like banners, inviting us to join them. When they saw we would not, they tied our gifts together in a shirt and left the bundle on the beach.

Paco and I looked at each other. He was as bemused as I was by this method of trading. He shrugged at me, and I shrugged back. There was nothing we could do but wait to see what would happen next.

A short while later we saw a canoe carrying an old man and two girls pulling toward the caravel. The Indians ashore were making signs to us—clearly we were to keep the girls. When they came aboard, the girls behaved pleasantly and modestly. One was about eight and the other about fourteen, and they wore their hair cut like ours. They showed no fear or sadness, and to my mind they were courageous in facing us, although we were completely strange to them in appearance and manners.

"They're so pretty," Paco whispered to me.

My father signaled him to keep silent. Although the Talamanca girls were gifts to us, the Admiral no more intended to accept them than the other gifts. He summoned Gonzalo Díaz and asked him to bring food and clothes for the girls.

While this was being done, the old Indian suggested in sign language that my father send a ship's boat to the mainland for water. The Admiral gave the signal, and our ship's boat headed for shore. The old man followed in his canoe, thinking, I am sure, that we were going to allow the girls to stay. But when our ship's boat returned with the water, my father sent the boat back to shore with the girls and the food, clothes, and gifts we had given them.

"I wonder what they're thinking now," said Paco.

"They must be completely baffled at this point. But I suppose the girls' parents are glad to see them none the worse for their trip," I said. "And from what I can see, the Indians don't look displeased with what we've done."

"The girls were sweet," said Paco, "especially the younger one. I wish we could have talked to them." His face had a distant look, and it slowly dawned on me why he was so interested in the girls. They must have reminded him of Caridad, far away in Spain.

The ships' boats went to Cariay again the next day for water; the sailors behaved politely so as not to disturb the Indians, who were there again with the girls, watching. The Indians returned the clothing and the other gifts we had given the girls. How much longer would this go on? I wondered.

The next day Uncle Bartholomew came aboard the *Capitana*.

"I've decided to go ashore to find out more about these people, Christopher," he said to my father. "They may be able to tell us something about gold. Do you have any objections?"

"Not now," he said. "I think we've made our peaceful intentions clear." He turned and looked at Paco and me standing nearby, listening. "Will you take the young men with you?"

I looked at my uncle, praying that he would say yes.

He smiled and nodded. "We'll also need a scribe," he said.

As our ship's boat approached the shore, we were startled to see the Indians scatter a powder in the air. Then, once the four of us were on land, two of the Indian men took Uncle Bartholomew by the arms and sat down with him on the grass to talk in sign language. Paco and I stood to one side and watched. The scribe who had come along with us sat down with the men and took out a quill, ink, and paper. Dipping the quill in the ink, he held it poised to write down the conversation. Suddenly the Indians leaped up and ran away, scattering more powder as they left.

Bartholomew and the scribe got to their feet. "No use," said my uncle. "They're afraid of being bewitched." The scribe headed back to the ship's boat, and we went up to my uncle, who was slapping his hands together to remove some grass clinging to them.

"That may be why they refused our gifts, sir," said Paco. "Perhaps they think we are sorcerers."

" 'A rogue sees himself in every other man,' according to the adage," I added. "For my part, I think they're the sorcerers. Why else did they scatter that powder in the air?"

"Perhaps it has something to do with their religion," Paco said.

Bartholomew nodded. "I've seen many Indians who burn powder in censers and wave the smoke around as our priests do during Mass. You may have a point, Paco. The powder might have some religious meaning to them."

I did not care for this sort of talk at all, and I broke in. "But the Indians have no religion. How can you compare them with us?"

Paco looked at me as if surprised. "I believe all people want the same things," he said. "They too must believe in something."

"But they're not Christians," I insisted.

"No, they're not. Neither was my mother, and many people could not forget that," Paco said angrily. "But she became a Christian and a good one, too. She was kinder and more loving than all our neighbors who shunned her in the name of Christianity."

Suddenly I felt ashamed. I had forgotten about Paco's mother.

Uncle Bartholomew spoke. "Don't argue, boys. Fernando knows that the Indians can become good Christians. Many on Española already have. Something else must be bothering you, Fernando. What is it?"

"I just don't like the Indies," I said flatly. "It's not civilized here. I wish I were home."

"I knew there was something," Uncle Bartholomew said. He put his arm around my shoulder, and we walked to the ship's boat. "You'll feel better later. All this is strange, and it takes time—a lot of time—to get used to it. I think part of the trouble is that you haven't really had a chance to get to know this country. If you were more familiar with the land and people, you'd probably like them better. Your father wants to learn more about Cariay, so tomorrow I'm going to explore the interior a bit. I think you— and Paco, if he wishes—should come with me. Agreed?" He looked at us, waiting for an answer. We nodded, I slowly and Paco eagerly.

I suppose my outburst—which had surprised me as much as it did Paco and Uncle Bartholomew—made me feel better, for the next day I found I was actually enjoying myself as the three of us walked through the forest. We followed a path, which looked as if it had been made recently. The woods were full of birds calling out in strange voices as we went by. The screeching of the parrots became annoying after a while, but some of the smaller birds sang as sweetly as nightingales. We saw one bird, as large as a peacock, which looked as if it were covered with wool. There were also gray cats the size of greyhounds climbing about like squirrels from tree to tree, using their long tails to grasp the tree limbs. They were amazing to watch, so swiftly did they move.

We had not gone far along the path when we came to something that took us by surprise: a large wooden palace, roofed with cane.

"What's this?" Bartholomew asked.

We went inside and saw several tombs. A dried and embalmed

corpse lay in one of them. "That explains the path," said Bartholomew. "Someone must have died recently and been brought here." In another tomb were two more bodies, wrapped in cotton cloth, and I swear there was no bad odor about them. There were some carved tablets hanging over the tombs, and we went forward to examine them. One had figures of beasts and another an effigy of a man; all were adorned with beads and other things the Indians prized.

"These surely are the most intelligent Indians in the area," said Bartholomew. "I've never seen anything like this before."

"It looks as if I was wrong about their not having a religion," I said. "Surely they must if they care for their dead like this."

We made our way back to the caravels without speaking, our minds full of the sights we had seen.

It was now early October, and my father began to get restless. We had lingered on at Cariay, delaying the search for the strait to the Indian Ocean, long enough. It was time we moved on.

"We shall need interpreters," he said to Diego Tristán one morning. Tristán nodded and gave orders to some of the men. They went ashore, and came back a few hours later with seven Indians in tow.

My father looked the Indians over and motioned two to one side. Through gestures he tried to explain that he wished them to stay with us as guides and would set them free later. Apparently, though, the other five, who were returned to shore, misunderstood him and thought that the Admiral wished to hold their two companions for ransom. The next day four Indians came aboard and offered various things, including two small wild boars, in exchange for the guides. My father kept one of the boars and sent the bewildered but amiable ransomers away with the other. The two

Talamanca guides remained with us, and Paco set about, as he had with Yumbé, to learn from them.

Later that day one of our crossbowmen brought us one of the gray creatures I had seen in the forest. I soon found out from a sailor that it was not a cat but a monkey. One of its front legs was missing—the crossbowman had had to cut it off because it was the only way to capture it. The monkey was a fierce little thing. It attacked all of us, including my father's Irish wolfhound. Then it caught sight of the boar the Indians had brought, and to our amazement the pig backed off in fear.

"Throw them together and see what happens," shouted my father. Juan de Noya carried out my father's request.

The monkey coiled its remarkable tail around the boar's snout, seized it by the neck with its remaining claws, and bit hard. The pig grunted in fear and pain.

We all laughed except for Paco. His face was sad as he watched the spectacle. A few minutes later he turned away and went back to work with the interpreters.

That night my father said he would write to the Catholic Sovereigns about this novel incident: he found it such fine sport.

As for myself, the incident meant only one thing. These strange monkeys must hunt other animals, as do the wolves of Spain.

XIV / *The Search for the Strait Is Over*

$\mathbb{A}$FTER LEAVING CARIAY, we sailed southeast along a fertile coast, searching for the passage to the Indian Ocean. The Talamanca interpreters had told us the strait was not far. By that evening we had traveled some fifty miles when we came upon an inlet which led us into a large bay. The Indians we met on the shores of the bay opened their arms wide and told our interpreters from Cariay that yes, there was a big sea nearby, and then pointed southwest.

When my father heard that the Indians called their land Quiriquetana, he began to wonder. The following day, as we sailed through a narrow passage between two islands, I could hear him murmur "Quiriquetana," turning the word over in his mouth several times as if he were trying to make it fit an idea he had. Finally he exclaimed, "Ciamba! This must be Ciamba."

I looked at him in surprise. "Ciamba?" I repeated.

"Ciamba is Marco Polo's name for a region in the Indies," he explained, growing animated.

"I remember now," I said. "It's between Cathay and India."

"That's right. By San Fernando, if this is that place, the Indian Ocean must be right around the corner." He slapped his hand on the railing in triumph.

Just then we came out of the channel and entered another immense blue-green body of water. Was this the strait to the southern sea? The next day when we landed on the mainland, which was surrounded by a tree-covered mountain range, we found that we were not offered pendants made of copper and gold. We traded our trifles for pure gold mirrors bigger than my face—not true mirrors, of course, but gold disks etched with strange designs. They shone like small suns, dazzling my eyes when I held them up to the real sun to catch its rays. We sailed in these waters for ten days. We received more gold; some of it was carved in the shapes of animals and birds we could not recognize, and so we came to call them all eagles.

Our interpreters from Cariay were intelligent and continued to pass along as much as they learned from the Guaymi, the people who lived in this region. We were disappointed to discover that, contrary to what we had hoped, this was not a strait but only a large bay, which my father called Alburemá, on an isthmus between two seas. The ocean lay, according to the Guaymi, nine days' march across the mountains. A province called Ciguare faced that ocean.

Through the interpreters we plied the Guaymi with questions, which they answered freely, so eager were they to please us. We were assured that the people of Ciguare had gold—much of it. Yes, they wore coral and used pepper. Clothed in rich garments, they fought with swords, of course—and cavalry—and even had warships equipped with cannon. We were on the Malay Peninsula without a doubt—or so my father said—and the Ciguareans were only a ten days' sail from the Ganges River. He was overjoyed to know that we were so close to the south sea and that all his calculations were correct. But what could we do about it? We had neither the strength nor the men to attempt the long overland journey across the mountains to Ciguare.

After the excitement of learning about Ciguare, my father grew thoughtful. "We shall continue sailing, Fernando," he said to me as we ate together in his cabin one afternoon. "Perhaps we may still find a strait, but I doubt now that one exists, since the Guaymi tell us that we can reach the Indian Ocean only by marching across the isthmus." He broke off a piece of cassava bread. "It would be better now to turn our attention to gathering gold to repay the Queen's faith." He bent his head and carefully wiped the bowl clean with the bread.

Gray hair hung lank to his stooped shoulders. He had grown older on this voyage. His face was thin, and his eyes looked sunken in their sockets. I could not bear to see him this way. He spoke not a word about failure, but I knew he was disappointed and no longer wished to talk about finding the passage. The search for the strait was over as far as he was concerned, and the less said about it the better. Still, I continued to hope.

After we left Quiriquetana, we continued down the coast and anchored at the end of the day at the mouth of the Guaiga River, where we stayed for over a week. As we found out later, we had come to the beginning of a region called Veragua.

Before we went ashore for the first time, we saw more than a hundred Indians on the beach. Splashing, they rushed into the sea and waved their spears at us. At first we sat quietly in the ships' boats, but when it became clear that this did not convince the Indians our intentions were peaceful, I jumped into the sea with some of our men and tried to assure the Indians with signs that we had come in peace. In return they spat some evil juice at us from a herb they were chewing.

Eventually we were able to calm them down and managed to trade some hawk's bells for sixteen mirrors of pure gold. But the next day, when we tried to trade again, the Indians rushed out with spears once more. Since talk got us nowhere this time, one of our crossbowmen shot an Indian in the arm. Then the men on the caravel fired a cannon, and the Indians ran for cover.

After that, the Indians saw they could not overpower us, and we traded, obtaining three more mirrors, which were all they had. The Indians told us they had originally come down to shore from their village in the interior to fight not to trade. We learned, too, through our interpreters, that somewhere in this region gold was mined in great quantities. My father was eager to pursue this news, and after a study of what he called the samples, the Admiral decided to sail on in search of the gold mines.

Some time later we anchored in a river near the village of Cateba, where we saw many people standing out in the open in a pouring rain, while their king stood under a huge leaf held over him for protection. After some lively trading, we had nineteen more gold mirrors, bringing our total of samples to almost fifty. It was here, too, that we saw the first true building in the Indies. A great mass of something like stucco, it seemed to be made of stone and lime. The Admiral ordered a piece of it to be chipped off as a souvenir.

We continued sailing east and came to five more villages of active trade. The fourth of these, like the region, was called Veragua, but since a sandbar blocked the harbor, we sailed on to the next village, Cubiga, which, we learned, marked the end of the gold-trading country and the region of Veragua. The night we left Cubiga we ran into a violent storm and had no choice but to go where it drove us. Fortunately, it took us to a beautiful harbor, which my father called Puerto Bello. We stayed there for a week, captives of the foul weather, and traded trifles for food and spun cotton.

It was November by the time we left Puerto Bello and came to a place the Admiral called Puerto de Bastimentos, which means port of provisions. The land and nearby islands were full of corn-fields cultivated by the Cuna Cuna Indians who lived there. We stocked our ships with food, staying for twelve days until the caravels—which were in sore need of repair—were fit for traveling once more.

Our next shelter from the storms—which seemed to be always against us in this season—was a small bay, so small it called to mind a closet, whereupon the Admiral named it Retrete. The Indians at Retrete were the best-looking people we had seen so far. They were tall and spare—not pot-bellied as so many Indians were—and handsome of face.

Because the ships lay so close to the banks, the sailors were able to sneak ashore easily during the nine days we stayed there. And this led to trouble. My father had made it a point to trade peace-fully with the Indians when possible, reasoning that in the long run it was more profitable to obtain gold bartered willingly than to fight for it. But our greedy and dissolute sailors paid no heed to my father's orders. Whenever they could, especially at night, they would quietly leave the ships, hopping onto the banks and disappearing into the woods. They would "buy" gold at gunpoint, steal food from the houses, and kidnap the women.

Finally the Indians could stand the sailors' depredations no longer, and one day they gathered around the ships angrily. The Admiral tried to placate them with promises, but the Indians no longer trusted us. They milled around the ships and glared at us menacingly. Since my father's words fell on closed ears, he decided that a show of force was called for.

"Fire the cannon," he ordered.

The cannon boomed, and a shot flew out of sight. The Indians began to shout and beat the branches of the trees to show they could make noise too.

"So, they think our cannon is only a noise-maker," my father said. "Fire again, but aim near that group of Indians on the hill."

The shot was accurate. When the Indians saw that our thunder carried a thunderbolt, they melted away into the forest and hardly dared peep at us again. Meanwhile, on the caravels, orders were shouted, threats were made, and our sailors found themselves confined aboard until we sailed. There would be no more trading at Retrete.

On our last day at Retrete Paco and I went for a walk with Juan de Noya. As I was about to step over a log, de Noya suddenly grabbed my arm and pulled me back. "Careful," he whispered. "Don't make a sound."

I looked at him. Had he gone mad? Then I noticed an odd smell in the air—it was if all the musk in the world were in one spot.

"Crocodile," de Noya said, pointing at the log, which slithered into the water.

"What was it?" asked Paco.

"Very dangerous," said de Noya. "If they find you while you're sleeping they will drag you into the water and eat you. Or so I've been told by people who have seen them along the Nile River in Egypt. Let's go back. It's too cowardly to attack us, but we're not safe here."

"It looked just like a log," I said.

"I didn't even see it," said Paco.

De Noya put his arms around our shoulders, and the three of us walked back to the caravel. "You're lucky I was with you. The Indies are full of terrible monsters. They say that on the island of Cuba there are men with tails."

"Now that's too much to believe," I said.

"It's true, it's true," de Noya insisted.

Paco and I smiled at each other and went on walking as de Noya continued telling his stories. Still, we had seen a log that could eat a man. Perhaps his tales were not so farfetched after all.

XV / *Coast of Contrasts*

O NCE WE LEFT Retrete and were on our way back
to the region of Veragua to look for the gold mines, I gave
up my last hope of finding the passage to India, as my father had
done earlier. We had been sailing for half a year and I was tired
of getting nowhere along this rough coast. Our ships were riddled
with shipworms, which bore holes in the wood; no sooner were
the planks caulked than new leaks sprang open. Thunder, lightning, rain, and a wind that could not blow without changing
drove us hither and thither without rest. We came to dread the
lightning for its fire, the air for its fury, the water for its waves,
and the shore for the reefs and rocks that reared up in front and
in back of us.

But these terrors abruptly disappeared when we were faced by
a new one, the thought of which still fills my soul with awe. One
afternoon a great waterspout, twisting and winding like a whirl-

wind, passed between two of our ships. Thicker than one of de Noya's barrels, a column of water rose all the way from the surface of the sea to the clouds.

We stood stunned at the sight until my father appeared on deck, carrying a sword and the Bible. "Repeat with me the Gospel according to St. John," he ordered, and the sailors who knew the words faltered along with him while he read fervently.

" 'His disciples entered in a ship and went over the sea toward Capernaum. And it was now dark, and Jesus had not come to them. And the sea arose by reason of a great wind that blew....' "

As I spoke the words with my father I stared at the waterspout twisting toward our ship. Suddenly I was speechless; it would swamp us in a moment. But then the words spoken by my father gave me courage, and I went back to reciting the ancient miracle with him.

" 'They saw Jesus walking on the sea, and drawing nigh unto the ship: and they were afraid.' " At this some of the sailors began to moan with fear.

Clasping the Bible in his left hand and raising the sword in his right, my father traced a cross in the sky and a great circle around the fleet.

" 'But He saith unto them: It is I; be not afraid.' "

The waterspout twisted away from the path of the ships, lifted, and disappeared into the clouds. We were saved.

The next two days were deadly calm. Great schools of sharks followed us unceasingly, circling the ships.

With Juan de Noya's help Paco and I attached a piece of red cloth to a strong hook at the end of a chain. Sharks will eat anything, I suppose, because we soon found ourselves hauling them aboard with no end in sight.

Gonzalo Díaz cut one open and began to laugh. He took out a

turtle and spun it across the deck to me. "What do you think of that, señorito? It's still alive."

"A good omen for you, Gonzalo," I answered. "Since you saved its life, it's yours."

He grinned as I spun the turtle back to him across the wet deck. "True enough. I think I'll name him Lazarus."

"Look at this, everyone," called Juan de Noya. He had slit open another shark's belly and pulled out the head of a shark. "This must be the head of the shark we threw into the sea half an hour ago."

"How can a shark swallow a head as big as its own?" asked Paco.

"The shark's head is very long," I said, and pointed to the mouth, which extended almost to the middle of its belly. "Look at those teeth, Paco!"

"I'd rather not." He shuddered.

"You know, don't you," said de Noya, "that, like vultures, sharks can smell a corpse miles away?"

"That's why decent people won't eat shark," I said.

"It's bad luck too," said Gonzalo Díaz.

Like Díaz, many of the sailors thought the sharks were an evil omen. Others thought them poor sport because they were so easily hooked. But we all did the shark the honor of eating it, for by that time the meat and fish we had brought from Spain were gone. And God help me, our ship's biscuit was revolting. What with the heat and the dampness, it was so full of maggots that many of the men waited to eat until it was too dark to see them in the gruel made from the biscuit. A few, though, were not so fastidious; they were so used to the maggots that they ate their gruel in broad daylight, not bothering to pick out the worms because they might end up with no supper at all.

Happily, at the end of that week we found ourselves in a pleasant harbor where the people lived, like birds, in trees.

"Perhaps they are afraid of the griffins that inhabit the country," I said to Paco as we gazed at one of the tree houses.

"You've been listening to de Noya's wild tales again," he replied. "More likely they fear their neighbors."

This was probably true, because all along that coast the people have feuds with one another.

Just before Christmas we left this harbor and, once again, ran into unsettled weather, which, like an enemy, seemed always to be waiting for us. The weather actually grew worse each time the Admiral altered his course. Because of these constant changes in the wind and weather the Admiral named this region la Costa de los Contrastes.

We continued southwest as best we could toward the village of Veragua, and finally, on January 6, 1503, Epiphany, we anchored near a river the Admiral called Belén in honor of the Feast of the Three Kings.

Part II

XVI / *Gold at Bethlehem*

BELÉN IS WHERE our Saviour was born, but this Belén, a river on the coast of Veragua, was where the last of the Admiral's hopes for the High Voyage received its death blow.

During our first two weeks on the Belén River my uncle did some peaceful trading with the Quibián, the cacique of the village of Veragua, which lay up the Veragua River, a few miles west of the Belén. I saw the Quibián one day—a strong and intelligent-looking man—when he repaid the visit by calling on my father, who gave him some hawk's bells.

Both rivers had sandbars at their mouths so that the open ocean lay on one side and a harbor on the other. But after he sent some of the crew to take soundings, my father decided it would be better to make the Belén our base, since the water lay seven feet deep over the Belén bar at high tide and was dangerously shallower at the Veragua.

But then, on January 24, the rains fell so heavily that the Belén River began to rise abruptly under the *Capitana*. Her anchor cables snapped, and she was driven hard against the *Gallega*. The two ships fouled each other and drifted rapidly and aimlessly downriver on the swollen current toward the bay, where we finally managed to regain control. But now a violent surf was flinging huge waves over the bar, trapping us inside the harbor.

The wind raged for another two weeks, whipping the water furiously against the sandbar. Not until February 6 was it calm enough for the ships' boats to cross the bar. On that day my uncle set off down the coast toward the Veragua River with the three boats and sixty-eight men. He was headed for the village of Veragua, where he intended to ask the cacique for information about the gold mines. If they were as rich as we had been led to believe by the results of our trading, my father told me, his plans to establish a settlement on the banks of the Belén would go forward.

A settlement! This was a surprise. As I watched my uncle's expedition cross the bar, I began to feel uneasy. The news about a settlement worried me, and the emotions I had been struggling against since my outburst in front of Bartholomew and Paco began to grow stronger. Not only did I still hate the Indies, I now believed the Indies hated me. More and more it seemed that this was no land for Christians in spite of the souls to be converted to the true religion of God or the gold and slaves that lay waiting.

I could see the Indies were beautiful. Nowhere else is there such a jeweled sea that captures all the colors of the aquamarine, turquoise, and emerald. But that was not enough. I longed for the quiet, pine-covered hills of Granada and the orderly life at court, where all that was beautiful in art, literature, and music could be found. While there I had taken the pleasures of polite, congenial society for granted. Now, after nine months of hardship and the daily company of rowdy sailors—which I had enjoyed at first—I realized that my heart lay back in Spain, even though it is cold in Granada in February, and one wants to do nothing but sit near a fire and dream of the spring, when yellow flowers bloom gently among the new grass and the almond trees drop their petals until the ground lies covered with a pink snowfall.

I was homesick and tired of new sensations, and it seemed there would be no end to our difficulties on this alien shore.

I could not tell my father how I felt, since he had, as he said, sweated blood to explore this country—not just for the benefit of their Highnesses but also for me and my brother Diego and all our heirs to come. It would break his heart if I were to denounce the Indies or even confess that I felt that the land had renounced us. And, to be honest, I did not want to give up Indies gold. So I was resigned to keeping my thoughts to myself and went on with the work as if my faith were still as solid as my father's.

"It's not easy to reach the mines," my uncle told the Admiral a few days later on his return from Veragua. "They're way up in the hills, and the terrain is so rough we had to cross the river more than forty times to get there." My father and I listened gravely, but Bartholomew was flushed with excitement as he spoke. "But there's so much gold the men could pick it up from among the roots of the trees. We had no digging tools with us and none of us had ever looked for gold in the ground before, but with the Quibián as our guide we had no trouble at all. That region is perfect!"

My father broke into a smile. Clapping his brother on the

shoulder, he said, "That's good news indeed. But what about the Indians? Do you think they'll willingly help us with the mining?"

"No question about it. After we left the area where the gold grows on—I mean under—the trees"—he smiled at his own wit—"we went overland to the Urirá River. The first thing the cacique there did was to present us with food. Then we bartered for some gold mirrors. Later the cacique from another village came along and traded more mirrors. Everyone we met was hospitable and friendly, and they all told us there are many more caciques eager to trade."

"That settles it," said my father. "You'll stay on here while Fernando and I return to Spain for more men and supplies with all possible speed. Our ships are about to fall apart, so we can't afford to be as leisurely as we have been till now." My father's face grew serious as he spoke. I knew he was wondering whether the ships would last out the long voyage home. The caulkers were already joking that the ships would soon be all pitch and no wood.

"Did you happen to see a better place than the Belén for the settlement?" my father asked next. "I really don't like that bar across the mouth of the harbor. Either the water over it's low or it's too rough for us to cross. You won't be able to move about freely with the sandbar in your way."

"I didn't find any place better than this one, Christopher," my uncle said. "We might as well stay here. Look, do you see that little gully that comes down to the west bank of the river—and that little hill in back of the gully on the riverbank? That's where we'll build."

Ill and exhausted as he was, my father could have had no better partner than Bartholomew. At my uncle's direction the town of Santa María de Belén sprang up within a few days—a dozen houses made of wood and thatched with palm leaves and a store-house for the weapons, powder, and food. To be on the safe side we stored the necessities of life—garlic, vinegar, cheese, and what was left of the wormy biscuit—aboard the battered *Gallega,* which was to remain behind when we returned to Spain.

While the men were at work, Paco and I took long walks along the driftwood-littered shore. One morning we came upon a group of Guaymi from the village upriver on the Belén. They were scurrying about among a rain of sardines on the beach. The fish were jumping ten to fifteen feet out of the water. Amazed, we watched while the men delightedly picked up the fish gasping and flopping on the sand. Later we sat and talked to one of the men who had apparently gathered all he needed. He showed us some of the hooks he used when the fish did not cooperate by flying so happily to the fisherman. The tortoise shell hooks had been fashioned by sawing them into shape with a stout thread. Paco, who had by now learned some of the Guaymi language, in-terpreted while the man told us about another way they had of fishing—which I thought was quite novel.

The men would row down the river from their village in a canoe, slapping the water with their paddles as they went. At the sound the frightened fish would leap right over the canoe, but before they finished their arc, they would strike a partition made of palm leaves and fall into the boat. In all my life I had never heard of fish so eager to be cooked! With fishing that good, Paco and I agreed, the men at Santa María de Belén wouldn't have any worries about food.

We left the man still sitting on the beach, wrapping his catch in leaves. When the men returned to their village, he told us, the fish would be dried in an oven; they kept that way for a long time.

I was, of course, interested in all the Indians we met, for I knew I would be asked many questions about them when I returned to Spain. But personally I did not find the Guaymi particularly appealing. Some of their customs were strange, to say the least—for example, their habit of chewing dry coca leaves and spitting out the juice; because of this they all had rotten teeth.

But Paco enjoyed the company of the Indians; he had spent hours talking to them. "If Spaniards are to settle in this country," he said as we walked back along the beach, "we must learn from the people who have lived here for so long. We wouldn't have to worry about supplies from Spain if we could accustom ourselves to Indian food."

"You sound as if you plan to stay in the Indies," I said.

"Oh, I don't know. I'm not sure what I want to do with my life. I'll tell you one thing, though. Being a sailor isn't for me— I learned that much on this trip. Sometimes I think I'd like to be a priest so that I could serve the people. But I don't have an education or any way of getting one. When you're an orphan, you don't have much choice." He sighed and shrugged his shoulders.

I wondered if my father would let me keep Paco as my servant after we returned to Spain. I would ask him about that later, I promised myself.

"I hope something turns up for you, Paco," I said. There was a glow in my heart as I thought of how pleased he would be to learn that I would like him for my servant. "But to get back to what you said about Indian food. Do you mean that we Spaniards should learn to like Indian wine? That stuff's made from corn and palmetto and who knows what else? It's nothing like good Spanish wine."

"The taste is different, certainly," Paco answered seriously. "But it's still wine. Haven't you ever had the wine they make from the mamey apple? Or that good, strong pineapple wine?"

"But none of it tastes like Spanish wine," I insisted.

"You protest so bitterly, Fernando, that I wonder if it's really the wine you object to at all," Paco said. "Could it be that you miss Spain? Are you homesick?"

"What if I am?"

"Oh, well, we're all homesick, even me. No wine is as sweet as the wine from our own country. I could drink a barrelful myself if we had one." We both laughed, relieved to know that we felt the same way.

"Come on," I said. "Let's find some of that chicha you like so much. You're right. It's not that bad. It's the Indies I don't like. And I suppose that if I had never known Spain, I could tolerate the Indies well enough." For a moment I almost believed myself.

I linked my arm through Paco's, and we walked back toward the settlement.

XVII / *A Beard Is Promised*

℮VERYTHING WAS READY for our departure for Spain, or so we thought. But, as always, we were at the mercy of the weather, and now that the winter rains were over, the water level at the mouth of the river had begun to drop. Before we knew it we were once again trapped on the wrong side of the bar, which had barely two feet of water over it. We settled down to wait, praying for rain to swell the river so we could leave the bay.

One day, while we were still waiting for a change in the weather, Diego Méndez, one of the men who had sailed on the *Bermuda,* approached my father. Méndez looked anxious. "I feel the Indians are up to something—and it's not good," he said.

"I know what you mean," the Admiral replied. "I'm getting suspicious of those armed parties that keep visiting the fleet. They say they're just passing through on the way to make war some-where to the west, but I'm beginning to think they're scouting us. I don't like the looks of it."

It was a gloriously sunny day, and as I sat on the hatch cover in the shade of the mast, I found it hard to believe that war was in the air. I could see the men walking about peacefully in Santa María de Belén. The Irish wolfhound, which was to be left be-hind with my uncle, was sprawled on the riverbank, biting his tail. As far as I could tell, the dog's absorption in his fleas seemed to be the most serious business on the shore. I looked up at Méndez. He was not very tall, but his bearing conveyed strength and purpose. With his hooked nose and narrow lips, he reminded me of a hawk that would not be deflected from its prey.

"Those damn sailors," Méndez exclaimed, pounding his fist into his other hand. "They're up to the same kinds of tricks they pulled at Retrete. I wish there were some way to keep them on board." He looked at me and grinned. "Put them in the hold and let Fernando sit on the cover. The way they molest the Indians can only cause us trouble."

"You know we can't lock up the men," my father said. His eyes were narrowed against the sun and his jaw was set. He had been much more like his old self ever since he had decided to have the Guaymi mine gold for their Highnesses.

"I have an idea," said Méndez. "Let me take some men and one of the ships' boats and scout the area. I'll report to you tomorrow."

"Done," said the Admiral.

A short while later Méndez and a group of men rowed off in the direction of the Veragua River.

The next morning Méndez came to the Admiral's cabin to report. My father was just getting over a bout of malarial chills, and he sat wrapped in a cloak, looking exhausted. I had been standing by in case he needed anything. As he listened soberly to Méndez's report his sallow face grew pale.

"We hadn't gone far before we came upon an encampment," Méndez began. "There were a thousand Indians at rough count—and all in battle dress."

"A thousand Indians in battle dress!" I exclaimed. "What did you do?"

Méndez smiled at me. "What else could I do? As coolly as if I were stepping into an inn in Seville, I went ashore and spoke to them."

"You know the Guaymi language?" I asked.

"Enough to find out what I needed to know. The warriors were waiting for orders to attack us, though I couldn't discover when. My men and I waited offshore all night in our boat and kept our eyes on the encampment. I knew they wouldn't dare attack Santa María de Belén while we were out there and could row east to sound the alarm. As soon as the sun rose, we hastened back. There's no doubt about it, Admiral. The Indians don't want us to settle in their country."

My father thought a moment. "You say you don't know when they plan to attack," he said finally. I could tell my father did not want to believe Méndez's news. "Go back and try to find out more."

Méndez left us alone in the cabin, and my father slumped in his chair. "Leave me, Fernando," he said. "I want to think."

Reluctantly, I went out on deck. The heat hung over the caravel like a shroud. It was another sunny day, which meant there would be no rain to swell the river.

By nightfall my father's chills had turned to fever. Complaining that his cabin was unbearably hot, he came out on the quarterdeck, where a cool breeze freshened the night air. It was there that Méndez found him when he returned. Méndez spoke to my father with such poise and confidence that I couldn't help but admire him.

"I took along Rodrigo Escobar," he began, "and we walked down the beach toward the Veragua. At the mouth of the river we came upon two canoes full of strange Indians—not the ones we had seen before. I spoke to them for a while and found out that the attack is to take place in two days. Instead of keeping the plans a secret, the men bragged to us about them. Well, what could I do? I forced them to take us up the river to the Quibián."

"How did you do that?" I asked.

"Gunpowder works wonders," he said tersely. "When we walked into the village, I announced that I had heard the Quibián was suffering from an arrow wound. 'I should like to cure it with Christian medicine,' I said boldly. At that, for some reason, all hell broke loose. The women and children began screaming and one of the cacique's sons came rushing out of the big house, cursing furiously. He almost ran me down.

"This was no time for us to get excited, you understand. So I sat down on the ground and brought out a barber's kit—mirror, comb, and a pair of scissors made from fine Toledo steel. I presented the kit to Rodrigo, who then proceeded to trim and comb my hair.

"You know yourself that nobody can resist a haircut—I don't know why, but that's how it is. The Indians gathered around and watched the operation, quietly and intently. It wasn't long before the Quibián himself came out of the house to watch, and he ended up having his hair trimmed too. He seemed pleased with the barbering and was delighted when we gave him the kit. His wound was healing, he said, and he declined our medicine. After enjoying a companionable supper with him, we finally left to come back here.

"The news is the same, Admiral." Méndez stood straighter as he spoke. "They're going to attack us—and soon."

My father turned away and looked toward the shore.

"There's only one thing we can do to ensure the safety of Santa María," Méndez went on. "From what I've heard it's the Quibián who doesn't want any Spaniards to stay in his country. I even managed to find out that when he took Don Bartholomew to the gold fields he showed him mines belonging to other tribes in the hope that when we began digging, his neighbors would take up arms against us. He's wily and dangerous. I say imprison him and his family until you can bring us help from Spain."

My father looked at Méndez and then nodded. "I don't want another Navidad. I left those settlers alone on Española in 1493, and they were massacred when the Indians took revenge on them for their abuses. But that was our first colony in the Indies. We know more now. Bartholomew will keep the settlers in line, though even he could do nothing if the Indians attacked en masse."

On March 20 my uncle Bartholomew set off with a band of men to capture the Quibián. He was gone for two days and so did not know what we learned before his return. When he came back, he was so triumphant and excited as he told his story that he failed to notice how weary my father looked, holding his hands over the galley fire to drive away the chills that had overcome him again.

"You are aware, Christopher, that Veragua is not a proper village," Bartholomew began. Even though I knew what I did, I could not resist listening to my uncle. There was time to tell him our news later.

"The thatched houses are scattered among the trees and are hard to see," he went on. "But I finally spotted the Quibián's house, high on a hill overlooking the river. I told my men to surround the house and keep out of sight; I didn't want to alarm the Quibián.

"I walked up and stood in front of his door with five of my men so that he could see we were not much to fear. The first thing he said—through our interpreter—was that he didn't want me to come into his house. As you know, the Indians don't like us to see their wives.

"Our interpreter was more frightened than anyone else. He had told me that he knew the Quibián wanted to kill us, and he was worried about what would happen to him if they should succeed. Still, he did his job well. Through him I said to the Quibián, 'Pray, tell me, sir, how is your arrow wound? I earnestly hope you are feeling better. Perhaps you will let me look at it?' When the Quibián came out of the house, I grabbed his arm and held him while four of my men made him a prisoner. The fifth man fired his arquebus, and at the sound the rest of the men came out of their ambush and encircled the house.

"There must have been over forty people inside. When they saw that their leader made no resistance, they came out and surrendered. These were no ordinary Indians. We had the cacique's wives and children and some of the most important men of the village. They immediately began to negotiate for their release.

"One of them said, 'There's a treasure hidden in the woods. It's all yours if you let us go.' Well, for once I wasn't interested in promises of gold. I had come to get the Quibián and now I had his whole family as well. Or most of them—some managed to slip away into the forest, but I knew I could get them later.

"At that point Juan Sánchez came up to me and volunteered to take the prisoners back to the caravels.

" 'All right,' I said, 'but don't let the Quibián escape whatever you do. He's the leader of this whole rebellion, and without him the others won't attack.'

" 'If I should let the cacique escape, Don Bartholomew, I would suffer you to pluck out all the hairs of my beard—one by one,' Sánchez said. 'Rest assured that we'll soon see you back aboard the caravels. Good luck in your search for the ones who escaped.'

"And so Sánchez left to come back here—where is he, by the way?" My uncle gave us no time to answer as he rushed on with his story. "Anyway, we found the area too mountainous and wooded to search safely. We saw no other villages and decided to come back. Look what I've brought you."

Smiling broadly, his face lit up like the sun, the Adelantado handed my father a leather pouch containing three hundred ducats' worth of gold mirrors and eagles. "Isn't that beautiful?" he asked, not really expecting an answer. My father set the booty on the deck. "And look what else. This is the gold twist the Guaymi wear around their arms and legs, and this is the gold cord they wear around their heads like coronets." He heaped the twists and cords into my father's arms. The Admiral looked at them for a moment, then laid them on top of the pouch at his feet. He kept one gold cord and handed it back to Bartholomew.

"Keep a coronet as a token of victory," he said, embracing his brother. "I so enjoyed seeing you happy at your success that I couldn't bear to break into your story with my bad news."

My uncle arched his eyebrows. "Bad news?"

"Juan Sánchez arrived with the captives last night. I don't know what to do with him—" My father hesitated.

"What happened? Is something wrong?"

"Let him tell you himself." The Admiral beckoned to Sánchez, who came forward. Holding his head high, his jaw pushed forward, Sánchez addressed the Adelantado.

"I offer you my beard, Don Bartholomew—hair by hair. The Quibián escaped, and it was my fault."

"No—it can't be. What happened?" My uncle stood stunned while Sánchez continued his story.

"We got into the boats and set off down the river. The Quibián sat very quietly. After a while he complained to me that the ropes were hurting his wound and begged me, as a Christian, to loosen them. Thinking he was a man of honor, I untied all the ropes except one, which I held in my hand.

"After that the trip was so uneventful I fell into a reverie without realizing it. When he saw this, the Quibián took his chance. He jumped overboard and sank like a stone. If I hadn't let go of the rope whizzing through my hand, I would've been dragged to the bottom with him.

"At the sound of the splash the other prisoners began to yell and bounce about. We didn't dare go after the Quibián. By now it was dark, and we couldn't even see whether he made it to shore. We decided to return to the fleet without him. The forty other captives are below deck on the *Bermuda,* well guarded. They won't escape."

"That's serious news, indeed, Juan Sánchez," my uncle said. "Pulling out your beard won't make it any better. You've learned a hard lesson, and I hope it doesn't end up costing us too much. I trust the men on the *Bermuda* will keep the chains fastened on the hatch more firmly than you kept the ropes on the Quibián."

Bartholomew turned to my father, who was still standing by the pile of gold. "There's nothing for it, Christopher," he said. "There's too much gold to leave for others to find. We'll stay as we planned. Go as quickly as you can so that you may return to us the sooner."

My father agreed, hoping that the Quibián had drowned and that the forty Indians held as hostages would prevent an attack on Santa María de Belén.

XVIII / *Rout*

I STILL CURSE that bar across the mouth of the Belén River: to think that a mere strip of sand could do so much damage! We were once again ready to sail, but the river was still too low, and rough waves were breaking on the bar, so that the caravels could not leave the bay. Finally, after days of waiting, it rained, and at last the water was high and calm enough for the three caravels to cross the bar.

No sailor—even one like me—enjoys losing a ship, and I felt sad at seeing the *Gallega* riding lonely at anchor near the settlement. If the Indians attacked, the hulk would not be of much use to my uncle Bartholomew and Diego Méndez, who were staying behind with seventy men. My stomach felt queasy when I looked at that little settlement and thought of those thousands of Indians who did not want the Christians to stay. Like my father, I prayed that our hostages would ensure peace, for we had learned that the Quibián was alive.

After we had said our farewells aboard the *Capitana,* we rode out about a mile. Something—perhaps Providence—made my father suddenly decide to send Captain Tristán, Juan de Noya, and some other men ashore in the ship's boat to fetch more water.

About fifty settlers were still aboard the *Vizcaína* and *Bermuda,* which were just outside the bar, making their last preparations before leaving the caravels for good. To the Indians on shore it must have looked as though all but a handful of us were finally sailing away. As I watched Tristán's boat rowing toward shore I suddenly heard, carried from shore on the wind, a noise that made my blood run cold. Yelling, whooping—what was happening? At last the commotion was over, and all seemed to be quiet. But that was nowhere near the end. For three days, as we rode at anchor, we could hear the sounds of battle off and on, and though I climbed up on the rail many times and strained my eyes, all I could see from the distance were puffs of smoke wafting over the trees. It was to be many long days before we could find out what had happened on shore, for the weather had turned foul again and we could not cross the bar.

Meanwhile, my father worried so about Captain Tristán, Bartholomew, Diego Méndez, and the others that he became delirious with a fever. At one point he came out on deck and swooned from weakness. He wrote about this incident later, and I set his words down here.

"When I first heard the sounds of that terrible battle in which we could do nothing and then heard that grim silence which followed, I climbed to the highest part of the ship and called out for help. None came, and exhausted, I fell asleep and heard a compassionate voice saying: 'O fool and slow to believe and serve thy God, the God of every man! From thy birth He hath ever held thee in special charge. He caused thy name to resound over the earth. He gave thee the Indies for thine own. He gave thee the keys to the Ocean Sea, which were closed with mighty chains. What more did he ever do for David or Moses, than for thee? Fear not, but have trust; all these tribulations are written on tablets of marble, and not without cause.'

"I heard all this but had no answer to give. I wept then for all my sins."

The Indies were truly destroying us. My father recovered from his delirium, but he was not the same man. Whether my uncle was alive or dead, I did not know. Our captain had vanished. I prayed, oh, how I prayed for the weather to change so that we could sail back into the bay. We moved the *Capitana* closer to the other two caravels, and waited together.

But then, like a fire to which oil has been added, our situation grew even worse. I shall tell the story as I later heard it from those aboard the *Bermuda,* below whose decks the Guaymi hostages were kept.

One evening, earlier that week, some sailors fell asleep on the hatch, and so that they could have a smooth bed, did not secure the chains over it. When the captives saw that the hatch was not locked in the usual way, they heaped ballast stones under the opening. Standing on the pile of stones, they forced up the hatch with their shoulders, toppling the sleeping sailors to the deck. They then raced for the rail, and in a trice were overboard and swimming for shore. At the noise some of the other sailors rushed to the hatch and slammed it shut to keep the remaining prisoners —mostly women and children—safely below. This time they fastened the hatch chains properly and settled down to keep a better watch.

They still had enough hostages to keep the Quibián quiet, they thought. However, the next morning, when the hatch was opened, the sailors saw a tableau of misery. Preferring to die rather than remain captive, the prisoners had hung themselves from the beams, bending their knees for room to swing. Now we feared the wrath of the Quibián even more. We had lost our last chance to strike a bargain for the safety of our settlement. The Quibián would have no reason to refrain from killing the men on shore once he learned he would never see his wives and children alive again.

The sea stayed rough, and our lives hung by the anchor cables. And the lives of the men on shore? Pedro de Ledesma, the pilot of the *Vizcaína,* approached my father with a plan.

"Sir, with your permission, a group of us would volunteer to swim to shore if the *Bermuda's* boat would take us as close as possible."

Such loyalty moved my father, and he gave his consent to the venture, risking the last of the fleet's boats.

Waves were breaking on the beach, and when the boat had come as close as it could to the settlement, Pedro de Ledesma boldly dived overboard and swam across the bar. When he returned, we finally learned all that had happened.

At the first attack the Indians had rushed out of the forest and showered the Spaniards with arrows. My uncle seized a lance and charged the Indians, getting an arrow in his chest in return. The other Christians joined in the fight, using the edges of their swords to good advantage. The wolfhound also did his part in punishing the invaders. After three hours of this the Indians fled, leaving one Christian dead and seven wounded. Thanks be to God, though my uncle's wound was painful, it was not serious.

During the lull after the Indians' retreat my uncle and Diego Méndez led the men in building a rampart with barrels and other materials on the riverbank. With their cannon behind this rampart, they were able to keep the Indians at bay, for the Guaymi were afraid to leave the forest while the cannonballs were flying.

And then de Ledesma told us what had happened after he arrived at the settlement. He had barely set foot on the sand when the men began to shout, "Tell the Admiral to take us away." "Get us out of this rotten place." "We won't stay here." De Ledesma turned to my uncle.

"What shall I tell the Admiral?" he asked.

"There's no use remaining at Santa María de Belén," my uncle replied. "The men are rotten with fear of the Indians, and they have threatened me and Méndez with mutiny. We can no longer talk away their fear. It would be best for us all to sail away."

"Where's Diego Tristán?" de Ledesma asked. "Is he safe with you? He never returned to the *Capitana*."

"Dead," said my uncle. "That stiff-necked Castilian is dead, and it was his own sense of what was right that killed him, the fool. What happened was this. He approached the settlement just as the attack began, and we hailed him to come ashore and help. He refused. The Admiral sent him to fetch water, he said, and he was afraid our men would swamp his boat in their panic, and the Admiral needed it. He stayed offshore watching for a while and then left us to go upriver with his men. There, they were ambushed by Indians. According to Juan de Noya—who is around here somewhere—Tristán got a spear in his eye and was killed, as were all the others. De Noya fell overboard and swam underwater to safety.

"You can imagine what it was like here when he brought the news," my uncle continued. "The men had already seen the corpses of Tristán and his men floating down the river while they were building the rampart. The sight of the bodies and the croaking carrion crows circling above struck the men with such horror that if a heavy sea had not been breaking on the bar they would have sailed away on the *Gallega* right then."

De Ledesma's account convinced my father that he had to abandon Santa María, but it grieved him. "As soon as the weather improves," he said, "we'll take the men aboard."

We waited eight more days, all the time praying that our anchor cables would hold. Finally, using the *Bermuda's* boat and a raft—which Diego Méndez built by lashing two canoes together—the men were able to transport themselves and their gear across the bar. They were so eager to leave that even then, with refuge in sight, they fought among themselves in order not to be the last on shore alone. Within two days the men were transported, my uncle was back aboard the *Bermuda,* and nothing remained in the little harbor except the rotten hulk of the *Gallega.* It was all over. At last we were to leave Santa María de Belén.

XIX / *A New Captain*

ON EASTER SUNDAY my father appointed the stalwart Diego Méndez captain of our ship in place of Diego Tristán. The two men embraced each other, and immediately began to discuss the route to be taken. They decided to sail to Española, for all were aware the ships could not cross the Ocean Sea in their worm-eaten condition. However, Juan Sánchez and the other pilots thought Española lay due north of Belén, and so when, at my father's orders, we set sail to the east, hugging the coast for safety, they began to grumble and even told the sailors we were heading for Spain. This agitated the men, but when the Admiral explained it was necessary to sail east before we could cross to Española, they quieted down.

At Puerto Bello we had to abandon the *Vizcaína* because she was shipping too much water through her planking, which was no better than a sieve. Cramped aboard the remaining two ships, we followed the coast for another one hundred twenty-five miles. Believing we had traveled too far east and were in danger of missing Española, the pilots and sailors insisted that we turn north. Though my father protested, he finally gave in to their demands, and on May 1 we headed north.

On the tenth of May we sighted two small islands, which we called las Tortugas because they were full of turtles—like the sea around them, which looked as though it were dotted with rocks.

A few days later we were at anchor on the south side of Cuba, at the Jardín de la Reina—a chain of small islands my father had discovered on his second voyage. He told me that we were in the province of Mangi, a part of Cathay.

Cathay, Cipangu, India—I no longer cared where we were. All I knew was that by giving in to the sailors we had ended up northwest of Española. I was hungry and exhausted. All that we had left to eat was rotten biscuit and oil and vinegar. The caravels were so full of holes that we had to man the pumps day and night to keep afloat. To make things worse, the *Bermuda* fouled us during a storm one night and broke our stem. We managed to disentangle ourselves with great labor and by letting go of all the ships' anchors save one. We lashed the *Bermuda* to the *Capitana* for the night. The next morning we found that every strand of the last anchor cable had parted except for one which would not have lasted another hour. Had it given, that would have been the end: the place was full of rocks, and we would have run aground. But it pleased God in His infinite mercy to deliver us and the *Bermuda*.

Six days later we put in at an Indian village on the coast of Cuba. Can you imagine two ships sailing in strange seas with only one anchor to serve them both? Whenever we anchored we had to lash the *Capitana* and *Bermuda* together. After obtaining some food from the village, we continued on our way, pumping water from the ships and praying for a surcease of our troubles.

We could not make Española directly from Cuba because of wind and currents, so the Admiral set course for Jamaica, hoping it would be the last stepping stone to Española.

By this time the water in our ships' bellies had risen so high it was almost up to the decks. When the pumps broke down, we used kettles to bail. The work was backbreaking, and each time I dumped another bucket of sea water over the side and watched the water rise in spite of all my efforts, I felt my heart break. All of us would drown if we stopped bailing even for a moment. The thought of sliding down into the water for the last time, the thought of eternal rest, the peace to be found rolling endlessly and silently on the bottom of that viridian sea was so alluring I was tempted to drop onto the deck and wait for the waters to cover me.

But something—faith in God, who had delivered us from so many dangers; faith in my father, who had never failed to find a shelter in time of need; faith, perhaps, in myself, simply because I had already survived so much—kept me slogging to the rail with the kettle in an unending, wearisome rhythm of toil.

It was daybreak on Saint John's Day when we made the harbor in Jamaica called Puerto Bueno. We could not stay, for there was neither water nor a village, but at least we had hope. It took one more day of fighting to keep afloat and sailing eastward before we reached another harbor, surrounded by reefs, on June 26. We went around the end of a reef and limped into the bay of Santa Gloria, unable to keep the ships afloat another moment.

At my father's direction we ran the ships onto the shore as far as we could on the tide. They were close together, and for the next several days we worked on them, shoring them up on both sides with timber and filling the holds with sand so that they would not move when the high tide rose almost to the decks. To live on the ships in some comfort, we built cabins with palm-leaf roofs on the decks and on the fore and sterncastles. Truth to tell, it was not only the thought of comfort that moved us to build lodgings on the ships. The Admiral did not want the men roaming the islands among the Taino Indians. It was vital that they remain friendly to us and that we be fortified against possible harm from them. For at the time the Jamaican Taino had not yet been subdued, and there were no Christians but us on the island.

God and good fortune favored my father again, though I know that his knowledge and skill also played their part. We were on the point of starvation when he sent Diego Méndez inland with a sword and three companions to make trading agreements with the caciques. There was not a crumb of wormy biscuit left aboard the caravels when Méndez came back. My father embraced him on the spot. Méndez had returned in a dugout canoe loaded with food and paddled by six Indians. The good captain had bought the canoe from a cacique named Ameyro, with whom he became fast friends, for the price of a brass helmet, a cloak, and a shirt. Méndez told us the Indians he had come across were friendly and kind, and they were eager to barter. My father placed two men in charge to divide everything equally among all aboard.

Since our men were confined and could not leave the ships to steal and commit outrages, the Indians remained well disposed toward us, for we traded freely and fairly. What we needed most was food for the one hundred and sixteen persons on the caravels, and we received it in plenty.

For one lace point we would get one or two *hutías,* the edible tree rats common in all the islands. We gave two or three strings of colored beads for a large cake of cassava bread, which is made from roots. We got almost anything we wanted—and kept the caciques happy—when we traded a hawk's bell or a mirror or a red cap or a pair of scissors. Thus we had provisions, and the Indians thought we were good neighbors.

We were well fed and contented now that we were on a friendly shore. The reef protected us from storms, and the sandy beach that faced us gave a good view in case trouble should come from the Indians. But we could not forget that we were without seaworthy ships and were many leagues from civilization. We had not the tools or craftsmen to build a new vessel. Although we kept watch on the sea for a passing sail, we had no hope that a Christian ship would happen to come our way, for there was no gold on Jamaica.

We were marooned.

XX / *Messengers to Española*

MY FATHER NEVER regretted choosing Diego Méndez as his captain, even though the men were growing jealous of the favor the Admiral was showing this man who had done so much for all of us. By July a plan for our rescue had been devised, and Méndez was my father's first choice for carrying it through.

"I hesitate to accept this responsibility, Admiral," Méndez said to my father when he approached him. "Of course I'm willing to try to make Española in my canoe, but I fear the men will stand in my way since they're in such haste to leave this island themselves. I suggest you put out a call for volunteers."

My father immediately did so, announcing to his officers, "We have decided to send a messenger to Española by canoe. Whoever wishes to take part in this mission, speak up."

There was silence. The Porras brothers, who were the most eager to leave, looked at each other warily. Cross the open sea in a frail canoe? Impatient as they all were to leave Jamaica, no one wanted to take that kind of risk. It was my feeling that Méndez did not wish to do so either, but with his usual courage, he volunteered. My father chose a man to go with him, for no one else would volunteer.

There was no time to waste. The men were growing restless, confined as they were, and at any moment the Taino might grow tired of feeding us. Rescue could not come too soon, we felt, and once Méndez had said he would go, we bent ourselves to the task of readying the canoe.

While the preparations were being made, my father retired to his cabin to compose letters for Méndez to take with him. First he wrote to his brother Don Diego, informing him of what had happened. Then he wrote a long letter to the Catholic Sovereigns, relating all that had occurred on the voyage, even to the story about the boar and the monkey. Most important, he insisted that the news of the gold mines in Veragua was the best that "ever was carried to Spain." He reminded their Highnesses again of the humiliation he had suffered when he was sent home in chains. He urged the Catholic Sovereigns to pay the balance of their salaries to his men, who had "passed through incredible toil and danger." The letter concluded nobly, and I set his words down as I remember them.

"I came to serve at the age of twenty-eight, and now I have no hair upon me that is not white, and my body is infirm and exhausted. All that was left to me and to my brothers has been taken away and sold, even to the cloak that I wore, to my great dishonor.... The restitution of my honor and losses, and the punishment of those who plundered me of my pearls, will redound to the honor of your royal dignity.... I cannot keep silent even though I might so wish. I implore your Highnesses' pardon. I am ruined, as I have said. Hitherto I have wept for others; now have pity on me, Heaven, and weep for me, earth! If it please God to remove me hence, aid me to go to Rome and on other pilgrimages."

Then he ended it, "Done in the Indies, in the island of Jamaica, on the seventh of July, in the year one thousand five hundred and three."

He signed it in his usual way.

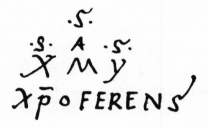

His last letter was a brief note to his friend Fray Gaspar in Seville. He asked to be remembered in the prayers of the monks at the monastery of Las Cuevas and added an ironic note to the effect that if the voyage had been as good for his health as it would be for the royal coffers, he would live for another hundred years.

Meanwhile Diego Méndez was working in haste. He took out the canoe he had bought from the cacique Ameyro, put a keel on it, and greased and pitched the bottom. He built up the bow and stern with planks to keep out the seas, and set up a mast and sail. The Indian dugout canoe is a strong vessel, but it settles three fourths into the water when loaded, and there is always the danger of being swamped. Méndez did all he could to make the canoe seaworthy, for the Taino do not take such long trips as he was going to.

Finally all was ready. My father gave Méndez the letters, and with one Christian and six Indians along, Méndez set out. We watched him until the canoe was out of sight, prayers for his safety—and ours—in our hearts.

To our great surprise he was back in a few days' time. My father was disappointed, but he said, "It's good to see you alive and well, Diego. What happened?"

"We ran into trouble with the Indians, sir. No, not our paddlers, different ones. We stopped at the northeast point of the island, our last anchorage before setting off across the sea to Española. When I walked into the forest, I was attacked by Indians, who clearly intended to kill me and steal the canoe. While they were drawing lots to see who would have the honor of killing me, I managed to escape."

"Will you try again?" asked the Admiral. "We have no other hope than your courage."

"Send a fleet of dugouts with me to that point as protection, and I'll continue. I would also advise that another canoe be equipped to accompany me to Española. It would double our chances of getting through."

In a short time another canoe had been prepared with Bartolomeo Fieschi, that good friend of the Columbus family, in command. And in a fleet of dugouts the Adelantado and a company of men set out with the two canoes to the northeast point.

There, with tears pouring from his eyes, my uncle told us after his return, he embraced the two brave captains. They agreed that when both canoes reached Española, Flisco would return to Jamaica with the news while Méndez pressed on to Santo Domingo.

It was dead calm when the two canoes with the Indian paddlers set sail, Bartholomew said, and he kept his eyes on the silent sea until the men who carried our hopes with them were out of sight. We settled down to wait.

XXI / *A Long Idleness*

THE HOT SUMMER DAYS at Santa Gloria passed. Many became sick because the diet of the island did not sit well with men who had endured so much hardship. But, thanks be to God, Paco and I remained healthy, and my father gave us permission to leave the ships when we chose.

At first we did not dare to go out of sight of them. We would walk from one end of the beach to the other and had many good discussions. To while away the time we would run races or collect shells, concentrating on one particular type—for example, the brown ones shaped like worms—and vying to see who could find the most. They were childish games, perhaps, but there was little else to do.

As we grew bolder, we would walk inland. Not far from the beach was a small hill, and we would go there and scan the

XXII / *"I Am for Castile!"*

"**S**IR, DO YOU WISH to keep us here to perish? What do you mean by making no effort to get to Castile?" Captain Francisco de Porras had entered my father's cabin without knocking and spoke to him insolently.

My father immediately guessed what was afoot but showed neither surprise nor fear and answered the captain calmly.

"I know of no way of getting home, sir. And I am second to none in my desire to leave this island. If you have a plan to propose, I recommend that you call a council so that we may discuss it."

"The time is over for talk," Porras answered. "Either you agree to embark now or you stay here with God."

He turned his back on the Admiral and shouted out the door, "I am for Castile! Who is with me?" I heard Juan Barba, one of the sailors, cry, "I am with you! Here is my sword." The voices of others joined his.

It was mutiny!

From the first my father had not trusted the Porras brothers, who were with the fleet not because of merit but because their sister was mistress to the High Treasurer of Castile, Don Alonso de Morales. Neither Francisco nor his brother Diego had ever done a fair share of the work of the voyage. My uncle Bartholomew had really commanded the *Bermuda*—without pay—and Diego had done nothing but count the gold as it was collected.

Although he was badly crippled and in pain with the gout, my father rose from his bed and left the cabin. Dozens of men were running about the ship, carrying arms and shouting, "Death to them!" "To Castile, to Castile!" Others had already occupied the castles and the crow's nests. The Porras brothers had plotted well; the ship was lost before my father even learned about it.

When his servants saw him standing at his cabin door, they rushed up to the Admiral and forced him back to bed. They were afraid that if he showed his face to the mutineers he would be killed on the spot. Then they ran to the Adelantado, who was facing the mutineers, lance in hand. They forced my uncle into the cabin with my father and pushed me in there with them. I was in shock, my mouth hanging open at the sight of such disorder and flouting of the law of the sea.

"By San Fernando," my father swore. "I shall have all the power of the law on those wretches. They will swing from the highest trees on Española for this."

"I think not, Christopher," said his brother. "They know too well that you're out of favor with Ovando; he'll protect them. They have their friends in Spain, too, don't forget. I fear we can do nothing."

"I want to go out and fight," I cried. The shock had passed. "Where's Paco? I must help Paco. I can't stay in here and listen to that bedlam outside. I want to fight." I was enraged that my father should be treated in this way by those foul traitors from the slums of Andalusia. I wanted to kill them all in as horrible a way as I could imagine. I wanted to see their bowels entangled on the end of my lance, their arms and legs thrown overboard to the sharks, their heads rolling on the decks as the seagulls fought over their eyes. They had betrayed my father. How dare they! My whole body ached with the desire for revenge.

And then it began to grow quiet outside the cabin. I felt fear stealing into me. Was everyone killed? What had happened to Paco? Were we now at the mercy of those murderers? I strained my ears to hear.

Wood bumped against wood. Then there were shouts: "We're off! We're off that rotten pig at last. We're off to Castile!" The mutineers were leaving the ship.

The cabin door flew open. It was Paco—alive. "They're gone," he cried. "All the traitors are gone." He pulled me out the door. "We talked them into leaving. Said it would be the best thing they could do because if they killed your father they would be punished by the Queen. Look"—he pointed toward the beach— "there they go." I saw ten canoes full of men paddling for shore on the high tide as if they were possessed. I laughed bitterly to myself: they had stolen the canoes my father had sequestered earlier and tied to the ships to keep the Indians from using them against us. I looked around the ship and saw that except for some loyal sailors like Paco, the only other men who remained aboard were those too sick to leave; there were many of those.

My father came out of the cabin and began to comfort his people as best he could. "Good riddance," he was saying. "We no longer have to worry about feeding that mob. Everything will be all right now."

My uncle followed him, shaking his head. Things would not be all right now, he knew. Not with those bandits running loose on the island.

XXIII / *The Heavens Help Us*

THE ADMIRAL took care to treat the Indians well so that they would not stop bringing us food, and the sick men on board gradually got better. From time to time in the weeks that passed we would hear news of the mutineers—and none of it was good. Later I was able to piece the whole story together from the reports of the mutineers themselves.

At first they were elated with the memory of their escape and the promise of freedom. They paddled to the northeast point of the island from where Méndez and Flisco had departed in July. On the way they committed innumerable outrages against the Indians they met. They stole their food, and as a further insult they told the Indians, "Collect from the Admiral. And if he doesn't pay up, kill the old man. You'd better kill him anyway— all the Christians hate him, and it's because of him that all the

Taino on Española are in misery. He'll do the same to you if you let him stay on Jamaica."

The Indians did nothing, for they did not know whom to believe: the insolent, disrespectful sailors or the man who had always treated them fairly and done them no harm.

After reaching the northeast point, the mutineers waited for a calm day and then set out in the canoes for Española, taking Indians along as paddlers.

But in January the weather is unpredictable, and they had not gone far when the wind blew up against them. They grew frightened and tried to turn back. Water began to ship in over the sides, and they lightened the canoes by throwing all unnecessary articles overboard.

The wind and sea grew rougher. The mutineers decided they had to kill the Indians and throw them over. After the first Indians had been killed, the rest jumped over the sides and hung onto the canoes. Pitilessly the mutineers hacked off their hands. In all they killed eighteen, keeping a few as paddlers. That was the Indians' reward for listening to falsehoods.

When the mutineers came ashore at the northeast point, they began to argue among themselves.

"Let's go to Cuba. It's closer."

"No, it isn't, you fool. It's on the other side of us."

"What do you know about it, you son of a Sevillian slut."

"Enough—let's go back to the Admiral and make peace."

"Are you crazy? Let's go back to the ship and kill them all."

"Stop it." A voice with authority finally spoke up. "Let's stay here and wait for better weather. Columbus wouldn't have sent his friends this way unless it was the best way out. Hey, Pepe— you—Jorge. Go find a village and get some food from the Indians. We'll wait it out here."

With this as their plan the mutineers made two more efforts to cross to Española and failed. Then they gave up and left the northeast point, heading toward us on foot, eating what they could find or steal.

Meanwhile we at the caravels found that the Indians were bringing us less and less food each time they came. Of course, they had no desire to work any more than was necessary, and one of us ate in a day what an Indian ate in twenty. By now they had all the lace points, hawk's bells, and caps they could want, and so we had to pay twice what we paid before for the same things—and feel grateful when they took payment. I'm sure, too, that some of them had listened to the arguments of the mutineers, which weakened our position and made the Indians feel they had no reason to go on working for us. They knew what they were doing and understood we were at their mercy. We were stuck on the caravels, where we might starve.

But God does not forget those who trust in Him, and He suggested a plan to the Admiral by which we might get all the food we would need. In his cabin my father had a handsome book printed in Nuremberg, the Regiomontanus *Ephemerides,* which predicted eclipses. He found that an eclipse of the moon was to occur before sunset on February 29, 1504—only three days away.

He summoned an interpreter and told him, "Go out into the island and call all the caciques to the shore. I wish to give them a feast and talk to them."

The interpreter departed, and the day before the eclipse the principal caciques of Jamaica assembled before us.

"My good friends," began the Admiral, "I have called you here to explain what we Christians believe." He paused to allow the interpreter to speak, and then went on. "Our God lives in Heaven, and we are His servants. He rewards the good and punishes the wicked. You saw how He punished the mutineers by keeping them from crossing to Española even as our friends, Méndez and Fieschi, passed safely. You well know how many trials and dangers the mutineers have suffered since they left this caravel."

My father looked out over the crowd, which was absorbed in the interpreter's words. The Admiral fastened his gaze on one particular cacique and went on, "God is angry with you." He swept his eyes over all the Indians. "He is angry because you refuse to bring enough food, which we pay for honestly. He will punish you for this sin against the Christians: He will visit famine and pestilence on all of you."

He stopped speaking for a moment, letting the words fall on the listening audience. The Indians looked at one another. Should they believe the Admiral? Was his God that powerful? More important, did the Admiral have power over his God?

"For those who do not believe what I say, let me tell you this: God will send a token to show you that what I say is true. Watch the rising of the moon tonight. She will rise inflamed with wrath, a sign of the wrath God will visit on all of you."

Some Indians gasped. Others scoffed. They fell to talking among themselves as they left.

Shortly before sunset the moon rose with the sign of the eclipse already on it. The higher it rose, the more advanced grew the eclipse. Even I, who knew better, felt a twinge of fear. At the sight of the half-eaten moon, red in the rays of the setting sun, the Indians began to scream with fright and came running to the ships from all directions. Many of them were laden with food and gifts, and they showed them to the Admiral, begging him to speak to his God and tell Him to be at peace, for henceforward, they promised, they would supply all the Christians' needs.

"One moment, my friends." My father spoke gravely. "I shall see what I can do. Excuse me while I retire to my cabin and speak with my God."

He left the scene and went into his cabin, where he watched the ampolleta sift away the half hours and made astronomical calculations.

The eclipse continued to eat the moon, and the air was full of the Indians' lamentations. When the Admiral had turned the ampolleta three times, he knew it was time for the eclipse to wane, and he went outside and spoke.

"I have appealed to my God and prayed for you. I have promised Him—in your name—that you would henceforth be good and treat the Christians well, bringing enough food and all else we need. God has pardoned you." The Indians were silent as they listened to the interpreter. "Watch the moon, and you will see His anger fade."

While the Indians looked on quietly, the moon grew large again. The tension relaxed. The Indians thanked the Admiral for his intercession and repeated their promises not to stint in supplying the caravels, for they did not know what caused eclipses and believed they were harmful. They did not suspect that men could understand what was happening in the sky. They knew only that our God looked with special favor on His servant, the Admiral Christopher Columbus.

As for my father, he had been able to calculate, because of the eclipse, that the sun sets seven hours and fifteen minutes earlier in Cádiz than in Jamaica, and that our correct position was latitude $18° 26' 45''$. Though we were landbound, my father never forgot that he was first and always a navigator.

XXIV / *A Slab of Pork &*
Two Barrels of Wine

T HE INDIANS kept their word after that, and we
had no more difficulty in getting supplies. Still, we were
hungry for Spanish food, and there was not a crumb of it about.
The men who had recovered their health were growing restless, and
Master Bernal began to hatch another conspiracy among the sailors.

It was now the end of March, and eight months had passed
since Méndez and Flisco had left for Española, and all we had
heard was a rumor that the Indians had found a big canoe floating offshore. We did not know whether this was Flisco's canoe or
merely a lie bruited about by the mutineers so that we would lose
heart. But the possibility that Flisco had perished on his return
to Jamaica further disquieted all of us and fed the conspirators'
desire to mutiny.

I could not understand how men who had been through so

much with the Admiral could turn against him. I especially regretted the defection to the Porras brothers of Pedro de Terreros,
he who had spoken up for my father when Governor Ovando had
insulted him at the time of the hurricane on Española; and Pedro
de Ledesma, who had swum across the bar to Santa María de
Belén; and Juan Sánchez, our pilot who had let the Quibián
escape. I can only think that such men of action were driven to
mutiny by their incarceration aboard the caravels. Men like that
cannot sit patiently for months, listening to reason when violence
seems the easier and more fruitful course.

It was Paco who told me of the Bernal conspiracy—he had
overheard some sailors discussing it—and I immediately reported
it to my father. "What shall we do?" I asked him.

"God has always come to our aid," he said, and then was quiet,
lost in thought.

I was impatient with this answer, but it turned out that my
father was right again. Our Lord did see the great danger we were
in, and He sent us a small ship.

"Méndez made it," I breathed when I saw the sails from the
little hill where Paco and I had kept our futile watch. We ran
back to the *Capitana,* arriving just as the strange ship anchored
beside her. We watched as a small boat was lowered and then
rowed across. I was beside myself as I saw the captain, Diego
Escobar, climb the ladder and present himself to my father.

"At your orders, sir," he began formally. "I bring the compli-
ments of the Knight Commander of Lares, the Viceroy of Española. He offers you his regrets that he has no ship large enough
to remove you and your men from this island at this time. He
hopes to be able to send one before long. Allow me to present
in his name this slab of salt pork and two barrels of wine." His
sailors set the wine and meat on the deck.

"I also have a letter for you," Captain Escobar went on. He handed it to my father.

The Admiral was as formal as Escobar, for he did not like him. He had been one of the rebels on Española and was no friend. My father thanked Escobar for the letter, and they spoke a while longer. A short time later Escobar returned to his ship; he sailed back to Española that same night.

The men groaned with disappointment as Escobar's caravel sailed away. Even Paco looked dejected. My father spoke to the crew immediately.

"Do not be discouraged," he began. "Méndez and Flisco arrived in Española safely, and a ship will soon be on its way here to pick up all of us. I could have left with Escobar," he lied bravely, "but I preferred that we stay together now that rescue is at hand."

He turned to me and Paco. "Open a barrel of wine," he said boldly. Then in a low voice he said to us, "We must pretend to celebrate."

When the men saw the wine pouring from the cask, they began filling their *botas,* the leather wineskins they carried over their shoulders. Before long they were singing the praises of Méndez, Flisco, Columbus—and Ovando.

My father motioned to my uncle and me. We went into his cabin. "By San Fernando," he swore. "I know in every aching bone of mine that Ovando really sent Escobar here to find out if I was dead. He wants me back in Española the way a cur wants rabies. Be still while I read Méndez's letter."

He read to himself; then he waved the letter in the air. "I was right. Méndez says we can expect no help from Ovando. Listen while I read." He read quickly, skimming over the letter to give us the high points.

" 'The first day out of Jamaica we had a fine calm and cruised all evening. From time to time the Indians refreshed themselves by swimming in the sea. By sunset we were out of sight of land. At night half the Indians paddled while we watched them for signs of betrayal. By daybreak all of us were totally fatigued.

" 'We urged on the paddlers, and took a turn at rowing ourselves. The Indians began to suffer the pain of Tantalus, who being in sight of water yet could not quench his thirst: they had been so feckless as to drink all the water they had brought with them the first day out because of the heat. By noon they were exhausted and suffering from intolerable thirst. We shared out a few drops of our water to keep them going until evening, when we hoped to sight the island of Navassa.

" 'They were discouraged, and thought themselves lost. That night one Indian died of thirst, and the rest were so weak they could hardly work at all. Like the vinegar afforded our Lord as He was dying, sea water was all they had to drink, and they wet their mouths with it. We passed through the night, and I shared out some of the precious water I had in my cask.

" 'By God's mercy the next morning we had reached Navassa, which was only a bare rock. Finding an abundance of rainwater, we filled the gourds with it. We warned the Indians to drink sparingly, but they filled their stomachs. Some died; others were made dreadfully sick. We cooked shellfish and rested for a day, and then pushed off for Española, reaching Cape San Miguel in the morning of the next day.

" 'I left Fieschi there with the Indians to rest before their return to Jamaica and took some men and headed inland to Xaraguá in search of Ovando. I found him, and he pretended to be pleased at my arrival. But I could not get his permission to proceed to Santo Domingo, where I might secure a caravel for your rescue. He was too busy suppressing an Indian revolt, and so far has had hanged or burned alive eight caciques.

" 'Finally he consented to my request, and I write now from

Santo Domingo, assuring you that a ship is being made ready to pick you up. I shall proceed to Spain with your letters as you ordered....' "

My father put the letter down and looked at us. There was nothing to do but wait.

XXV / *A Phantom Caravel*

LIFE CONTINUED to go on after the departure of the caravel. The Indians were bringing us food regularly, and we were healthy and in good spirits at the thought of rescue. I feared for Flisco, but my father assured me he was in God's care, and we would see him again. The Bernal conspiracy aboard the caravel had ended with the arrival of Escobar, but the mutineers led by the Porras brothers were still rebellious, wandering all over the island and stirring up trouble.

Before the ship Méndez was sending arrived, the Admiral decided, he had to make an effort to bring about peace. Accordingly, he dispatched two men with instructions to say that the Admiral was willing to grant a pardon to the mutineers. The messengers carried a generous slice of the salt pork as a token of the Admiral's good will and as proof that the Escobar caravel had indeed arrived.

When the messengers reached the mutineers' camp, Captain Francisco de Porras came out alone to meet them, for he did not want his men to hear what the Admiral had to propose. Porras was afraid his men might urge him to accept a pardon and end the mutiny.

After he had heard them out and accepted the gift, Porras told the messengers, "We have no reason to trust the Admiral. If he wishes us to join him, he must give us a ship of our own if two caravels arrive; if only one is sent, we want half the space set aside for our private use."

One of Porras's trusted lieutenants, who had joined him, broke in, "You know, we lost all we had when we tried to get to Española in those rotten canoes of the Admiral's. We won't go back to the caravels unless he gives us half of all the food and clothing."

The messengers began to protest that these conditions were impossible to accept, but the mutineers did not allow them to finish.

"If he doesn't do as we say," declared Francisco de Porras, "we'll march on the caravels and take what we want by force."

At that the messengers knew they could not even bargain, and so they left. But before they were out of earshot, they heard Francisco de Porras say to the other mutineers, "You can't trust that Admiral. He'll get even with all of you if you go back to him. We—my brother and I—we have nothing to worry about because we have friends at court. But you fellows—well, if you go back, you'll be taking quite a chance. Don't say we didn't warn you."

"What about that ship we saw come in?" asked one of the mutineers who had not been shown the salt pork.

"That was no ship, you ninny. It was one of the Admiral's tricks. You know he practices black magic; he conjured up a phantom caravel to fool you. If that were a real caravel, don't you think he'd have been the first to sail away on it?

"Listen to me, I know what I'm doing. For God's sake, without me to pull you by the noses, you'd all be finished. Let me tell you what we're going to do now. We're going to march on those caravels with the sand bottoms and take what we want. Anyone who wants a share, follow me!"

The messengers had heard enough. They hurried back to the caravels and warned the Admiral about the attack. Quickly my father called Bartholomew and told him what was going on. My uncle immediately left the ship and marched with fifty bold and trusted men to a hill near the village of Maima, where the mutineers had already gathered.

As he later told us, he decided to try again for peace without bloodshed and sent out the two messengers who had spoken to the mutineers earlier. But the mutineers were determined to fight, and they paid no attention to the messengers. Six of the mutineers had decided ahead of time to kill Bartholomew, calculating that once he was slain, the rest would come to terms.

"Kill! Kill!" they cried as they rushed up to my uncle, who was standing with his lance at the ready. But it turned out that God's plan was different from that of the mutineers. At the first clash five or six of the mutineers were struck down, most of them from the gang that had marked off my uncle for themselves. My uncle was no mean fighter. He was so angry when he heard the mutineers calling the Admiral's men cowards because they had been unwilling to shed blood on the day of the mutiny that he fell upon the traitors with all his fury. Before long Juan Barba, the first mutineer to draw his sword, Juan Sánchez, and Pedro de Terreros lay dead; many men were badly wounded; and Francisco de Porras was a prisoner.

"Who are the cowards now?" yelled my uncle as the remaining

mutineers ran off. "After them," he cried to his lieutenants, blood dripping from a cut on his hand.

But they restrained him. "Stop—let the traitors go. They deserve to be punished, but let's not go too far. If the Indians see us killing one another, they might decide to murder whoever wins."

"My blood is up," said my uncle. "I want to kill every one of those traitors. But you're right. We'll return to the caravels with our prisoners. At least we've got Porras, and without him to egg them on, they'll be quiet."

My father was overjoyed when he learned how the battle had turned out, though his brother's wound worried him.

"It's nothing, Christopher. Just a scratch. This and the feeble lance stroke your chief waiter suffered are the only injuries to report."

"Thanks be to God," said the Admiral.

Meanwhile, as we found out later, Pedro de Ledesma lay wounded at the foot of the cliff over which he had fallen, and the other mutineers did not know where he was. The Indians found him, and curious to know how our swords cut—or perhaps wondering whether Christians bled as they did—they opened up his wounds with little sticks and examined them. His head was wounded so badly that his brain was exposed; his shoulder was ripped open, so that his arm was hanging loose; one leg was cut from thigh to shinbone, and the sole of one foot was sliced from heel to toe so that it resembled a slipper. The Indians angered him with their poking, and he growled at them, "Get away from me or I'll kill you!" When they heard this from a man who by all appearances should have been dead, they grew alarmed—perhaps the Christians were indeed gods?—and left him alone.

When the other mutineers found out where de Ledesma was, they picked him up and carried him to a nearby hut. Since they had no turpentine, they had to use oil to cauterize the wounds. That, together with the dampness and mosquitoes in the hut, should have ended de Ledesma's life. "I swear I never saw so many wounds," declared Master Bernal, who had joined the mutineers after his conspiracy had failed. "I found new ones every day." In spite of this de Ledesma recovered in the end. But who can explain why my father's chief waiter, the one whose wound was so slight, died?

Left without their leader, the mutineers finally approached the caravels and begged the Admiral for mercy. My father granted a full pardon to all except Francisco de Porras, whom he kept in irons to prevent new rebellions.

As there was neither room nor food enough to keep the band of mutineers on the caravels, my father placed them under the charge of one of his own men. They were ordered to tour the island, trading peaceably with the Indians, until the caravels from Santo Domingo arrived.

It was May 20, almost a year since the *Capitana* and *Bermuda* had been beached on Jamaica.

XXVI / *The Scorpion's Kiss*

A SHIP ARRIVED a few days later, and we all joyfully embarked for Santo Domingo. Because of contrary winds and currents, we had considerable difficulty on the way, but we reached our much-longed-for destination at last on August 13.

Governor Ovando received us hospitably and took the Admiral into his own house. But this was a scorpion's kiss, for at the same time he set Captain Francisco de Porras free, without punishing him for leading the mutiny. He even proposed to arrange matters with the Crown so that those who had imprisoned Captain Porras would themselves be punished! So his smiles and hospitality toward my father were only a pretense, as my father knew from the beginning, for he had already suffered much from the hypocrisy of men's justice.

We passed the rest of the summer in Santo Domingo, waiting for suitable ships to arrive from Spain. I had not seen much of

Paco since we landed, and I had no idea where he had disappeared. But one afternoon we met by chance in the dusty plaza in the center of Santo Domingo.

"It's so good to see you," I said warmly. Indeed I was glad to see him. I looked at him carefully. His face grew serious when I asked, "Where have you been hiding yourself? I've missed you."

"I haven't been hiding, Fernando," he answered gravely. "I've been working. I didn't know how to tell you, but I'm not going back to Spain."

"You're not?" I said. "I had hoped—"

"If you reflect on it, my news ought not to surprise you. We've spent many hours thinking and talking about my future. I like the Indies very much, as you know, and there's nothing in Spain for me except my sister."

He took my arm, and we left the plaza and walked toward the harbor. Paco looked out at the sea and went on.

"Shortly after we arrived in Santo Domingo, I learned from your father of a planter who had need of Christian workers. When I told him I could speak some Indian languages, he took me into his house to work and learn. This man, Bartolomé de las Casas, is just and kind. I want to stay with him, Fernando."

He looked into my eyes and stood very straight. I could do nothing but believe him. Tears stung my eyes. I loved my friend and did not want to lose his company, but I knew he was right to do what he wanted.

"I have a favor to ask, Fernando," he said. "When you return to Seville, will you look for Caridad at the inn and give her a letter? She can't read, but perhaps you could read it to her and tell her what it's like in Española. I want her to join me. As a poor woman in Spain, she'll never be anything more than a drudge. Here she would have opportunities. There's a need for Christian women on this island; perhaps she'll marry a settler. If you can, arrange for her passage. Don Bartolomé is lending me the money for it. Say you'll do this for me."

"Why not? Of course I will, Paco. I'm going to miss you, but perhaps someday I'll return and we'll meet again. Until that time, take this." I gave him a small wooden cross I had carved during our stay on Jamaica. "And remember me in your prayers."

He took the little cross. We embraced each other, and I could see that his eyes were wet too. With his hands on my shoulders, he stepped back and looked at me. "I'll always carry this, Fernando," he said. "I wish you and your family good fortune, and I hope that some day you'll return to the Indies. I must leave now. I'll see you again with the letter and the money for Caridad before you depart."

He turned and ran off. I walked slowly back to Viceroy Ovando's house to tell my father what had happened.

"It was to be expected, Fernando," my father said. "These are new times, and nothing will be as it was before we Christians sailed across the Ocean Sea. Many men, like Paco, are remaining here. Although they give different reasons, they all feel that a new world is waiting for them." I learned later that several of the men who stayed behind became the first settlers in the colony of Puerto Rico. My father was right—these were new times.

We sailed away finally on September 12 in a ship my father chartered. The homeward voyage was beset with difficulties—our mainmast broke into four pieces during one storm and our foremast was sprung in another—but with their usual ingenuity and resourcefulness, the Admiral and my uncle, the Adelantado, saw to it that we crossed safely.

On November 7, 1504, we arrived at the port of Sanlúcar de Barrameda in southern Spain, and the High Voyage was at an end.

Epilogue / *Seville, February 9, 1536*

THE MESSENGER is waiting outside to take this manuscript to Italy, where it will be left with our bankers in Genoa. Will it ever see the light of day? No matter, when I hear that these childish jottings of the High Voyage are safe, I will write the whole story of my father's life to counteract the lies that are being published about his origins, his knowledge, and his voyages. Who would have imagined that the Holy Inquisition would find my innocent little tale written all those years ago to be seditious and prohibit its publication in Spain? I cannot believe how much power my Queen turned over to her confessor, Torquemada, in her lifetime. Scholarship has languished in Spain under such repression, and I wonder what will happen when I am gone to the wonderful library of fifteen thousand volumes I have so carefully amassed over the years.

But let me record briefly what happened after our return from the High Voyage so that the record will be complete.

My beloved Queen died a few weeks after our return to Spain. Although my father tried to see her in Segovia when he heard she was dying, King Ferdinand refused to grant him permission to make the journey. Nor would he ever restore my father's rightful privileges as Viceroy and Governor-General of all the lands he discovered.

Flisco, who had returned to Spain after his paddlers refused to take him back to Jamaica, witnessed my father's last will and testament. His heart broken, my father followed his Queen on May 20, 1506. His bones were interred in the monastery of Santa María de las Cuevas, here in Seville.

My old friend Paco prospered under the tutelage of the planter, Bartolomé de las Casas. He has an Indian wife and two little girls—Fernandina and Caridad—and seems happy enough being a teacher and small farmer. I saw him for the last time in 1509, when I went to Santo Domingo with my uncle Bartholomew and my brother Diego, who was its governor (but without the title of Viceroy!) for a while.

Diego died in 1526, and his wife, Doña María. de Colón y Toledo, a cousin of the King, renounced her claims to the titles, revenues, and privileges due Diego, as the heir of Christopher Columbus, in exchange for the Duchy of Veragua, a tiny speck on a continent that by right of discovery was ours to govern and receive income from. Perhaps she was wise to do so since it seems the Crown will never restore what it had granted to my father and then took away. Diego and Bartholomew tried hard enough to regain our just rights after my father died, but the Crown insisted that it had never intended to grant an entire continent to be ruled by my family, even though we have papers proving otherwise.

There are still many lawsuits relating to the first voyage plaguing the family, and countless falsehoods about my father circulate through the city. Greed dominates everything in Spain today, even as gold continues to pour in from her dominions. And if there is gold, there will be lawyers and upstarts until it is gone.

I much prefer the comfort of Seville to that rough colony Paco loves so much, even though it was the cause of Caridad's death. She married a settler, as expected, but lost one child after another to sickness, and finally succumbed herself. It is clear that her husband had infected her with the syphilis he had caught from an Indian woman before his marriage. So many Indians and Spaniards died on Española—God's revenge on the godless—that the island became little more than a charnel house.

And now Paco's old benefactor, Bartolomé de las Casas, is a notorious champion of the Indians' right to be free, while I, like my father, believe it is the Indians' duty to serve God and their Spanish masters. Las Casas gave up his plantation on Española to take up holy orders under the influence of Dominican friars who went to Santo Domingo in 1510. When last I heard, he was somewhere in Nicaragua, actively opposing the Governor's slave raids and marches of conquest. The land is becoming desolate and depopulated, he says, owing to fifty thousand Indians being sent to Panama and Peru as slaves.

As for me, I am content in my fine house with my books and visits from learned men. I have traveled a good deal on the continent, and I continue to learn. When I die my books will go to a new library at the cathedral of Seville. I have said in my will that they must be available to all scholars but only from behind a screen with an opening large enough for one hand to enter to turn the pages. It is impossible to preserve books though they be chained with a thousand chains, and I must trust in God that the library will survive.

The servant has come to tell me that the messenger grows impatient. I must end now. The full story of the Admiral's life waits to be written, and I will begin tomorrow.

Author's Note

Fernando Columbus died in Seville on July 21, 1539, and was entombed in the cathedral of Seville. During the last years of his life, he wrote *The Life of the Admiral Christopher Columbus,* on which a good deal of this novel, *The High Voyage,* is based. After his death, the manuscript of the biography was sold by an impecunious relative to a Genoese physician, Baliano de Fornari. The work was translated into Italian by Alfonso Ulloa, a Spaniard, and published in Venice in 1571. The original manuscript in Spanish has been lost. I am indebted to Professor Benjamin Keen for his translation of *The Life of the Admiral Christopher Columbus by His Son Ferdinand* into English, published by Rutgers University Press in 1959.

I have also relied on the monumental and engrossing *Admiral of the Ocean Sea* by Samuel Eliot Morison. *The Caribbean As Columbus Saw It* (coauthored by Morison and Mauricio Obregón), together with Bradley Smith's *Columbus in the New World,* provided me with a visual picture of the Caribbean to complement my own memories of travel in that area.

The Age of Reconnaissance by J. H. Parry was indispensable for information about European explorations in the fifteenth and sixteenth centuries, as was a visit to the Museu de Marinha in Lisbon, which has an excellent collection of model ships of the time.

Other writings that helped me include the abstract of Columbus's lost journal by Bartolomé de las Casas, *Personal Narrative of the First Voyage to America,* translated in 1827 by Samuel Kettell "from a manuscript recently discovered in Spain"; Paul Leicester Ford's 1892 edition of *Writings of Christopher Columbus: Descriptive of the Discovery and Occupation of the New World;* and *The Life and Writings of Bartolomé de las Casas* by Henry Raup Wagner with the collaboration of Helen Rand Parish.

And I am deeply grateful to Edward Babun, Caroline Lalire, George Nicholson, and Cary Ryan for their many suggestions and unstinting encouragement.

So much of what Fernando Columbus knew has changed in the past years. But the Patio of the Lions in Granada and the crooked streets of Seville are still there, evoking the past of a country to which those of us who call the Americas home must be grateful. At the same time, the story of greed and corruption underlying *The High Voyage* should also be noted, for it marked one more step along the road of a brutal conquest that destroyed so many native American peoples and cultures, a tragic loss for us all.

The events described in *The High Voyage* are as faithful to the truth as fictional liberties permit; with the exception of Paco and Caridad, the people were real. It is my hope that they live again on paper.

About the Author

OLGA LITOWINSKY was born in Newark and lived a good part of her life in Belmar, New Jersey, one block away from the Atlantic Ocean. She is a graduate of the Latin American Institute and Columbia University, with honors in history. Currently she is an editor with a major New York publisher. She is the author of *The Dream Book* and *Oliver's High-Flying Adventure*.